NINE LIVES

Tom Gumbert
&
April Kautzman

ALL THINGS
THAT MATTER
PRESS

Prologue

 Have you ever looked at a shooting star and wondered where it came from, how far it has traveled, and how much farther it has yet to go before its journey ends? I never really considered the myriad of possibilities that exist in the universe until recently. How small and insignificant we oftentimes feel and yet how epic we truly are, or *could be,* if we just allowed ourselves to believe; to believe that we all exist in this world for a purpose. I have come to believe that my time spent on this earth was for a purpose greater than I myself could ever have imagined.

I am a cat.

Cats have been on this earth a very, very long time: twelve million years in our current familiar form. According to most human experts, we first appeared here thirty million years ago.

We are widely regarded as mysterious, independent, vital, and loveable. We have inspired awe and reverence as well as fear and loathing, and our mystique has resulted in humans both worshipping us as "gods" and exterminating us as "agents of Satan." I assure you we are neither.

It has often been said that cats have nine lives. That conjecture comes from our ability to get out of precarious situations, to land on our feet after a fall, to avoid disaster when it seems unavoidable. All of these things are, of course, true. But it is also a literal statement of fact. We cats have been given the ability to reincarnate. I'm not sure how this mysterious gift works, only that I have been born and re-born multiple times and that my lives are part of a journey that has crossed many centuries.

Until recently I was unaware of the Great Gift, as I have come to call it. Not until I reached the end of my journey, the end of my existence in this world, did it make itself known to me. Only in this last life did the shroud lift and I remember the details of my previous lives. I accept this as the way of the Great Gift, but I still wonder if I would have lived my lives differently if I'd had this knowledge. Perhaps that is why it is kept from us until the very end. Perhaps it is so that we may live our lives without past regrets weighing down upon us or coloring our choices.

Most time I just *was*, an ordinary creature with ordinary wants and needs and yet my life intertwined with those who were themselves unique and wondrous, even if they did not recognize that truth.

You see, each life *does* have a purpose, even the life of a cat. The purpose may be to keep control of the rodent population in a given area so that humans do not starve. It may be to bear witness and help carry the message across the decades of lessons learned. It may be to simply serve as a companion. It may even be to participate in events that transcend the ordinary, lifting them to the truly extraordinary.

At the end of this life I know that I have served my Creator faithfully and I feel no sorrow that my journey is ending. I have seen much senseless violence and have had my share of pain and heartache. I have also lived well and loved well, so I am content. I have only one thing left to do and that is to share my journey with those who would care to listen.

Chief Dan George, a very wise man, once said, "If you talk to the animals they will talk with you and you will know each other. If you do not talk to them you will not know them, and what you do not know you will fear. What one fears one destroys."

Talk with me so that I may share my journey with you and we may know each other.

Walk with me…

Life One ~ Til Death Do Us Part

The mist from the great river lifts as the sun heats the morning air. Bubastis is busy with traders, farmers, and merchants, and they nod and smile at me with great respect as I trot from the riverbank where I quenched my thirst after having devoured a rodent that was eating the royal grain.

My curiosity almost cost me my life as I peered at a group of children and didn't see the on-coming cart that the laborer was pushing. Luckily, he swerved to avoid me, almost upsetting his cart. You would think he'd be furious at me but instead he is visibly relieved and mutters a prayer of gratitude to Bast. I then remember the law: it is forbidden to take the life of a cat, even by accident. Anyone breaking the law is punished by death.

There is great excitement today as it is the annual celebration of the Festival of Bast. Throughout the day throngs of people will make their way to the temple of Bubastis singing, playing music, clapping their hands, and drinking wine. The merchants sell items to be offered as a sacrifice to Bast, the half human/half cat goddess of fertility, motherhood, grace, beauty, joy, music, and dancing.

It is May in the year 455 BC and the Egyptian sun, like the goddess being celebrated, is at its gentlest. Its rays warm but do not burn me and I become sleepy and look for a nice spot in the reeds to take a nap.

When I awake, the sun is in the afternoon sky and I am famished. I work my way through the reeds along the bank of the great river they call Nile until I see some moving slightly against the direction of the wind. Keeping low to the ground, I creep close enough to see my dinner: a water snake. I coil into a crouch and spring forward, pouncing on the head of my victim. I hold it pinned to the ground with my claws as it frantically tries to twist away from my clutches. I sink my teeth into the area behind its head and crush its throat, making very quick work, if I do say so myself.

After satisfying my hunger, I clean myself until at last I am drawn by the sounds of people arriving at the dock. I make my way to the landing area before I stop to watch visitors arriving as they are drawn to the city by the festival. Today, nearly seven hundred thousand people will participate in the festivities.

The people arrive in groups of twenty or thirty. The mood is festive, bordering on outrageous. The conversation is an interesting mix of religious piety and mating ritual, befitting the nature of the festival.

As I wander through the city, I notice that the children, who would normally be out en masse on such a fine day, are not playing in the streets. In fact, their mothers are escorting the few I do see home, as children are forbidden to participate in the Festival of Bast. Even though I will miss my little friends, I think this is a good idea as the rituals and general mood of the festival are adult in nature and usually become quite rowdy.

Evening is quickly approaching and the thoughts of most humans turn to dinner. Tonight they will feast. In addition to the daily staples of breads, beans, pomegranates, figs, cucumbers, radishes, and cabbage, tonight the masses will enjoy a variety of fish, fowl, and the meat of grazing animals such as cows and goats. They will wash down this feast with fermented drinks of beer and wine.

As more wine is consumed, the language of the crowd becomes increasingly ribald and women, freed from their inhibitions, are seen raising their skirts to entice men into the act of consummation. For most, it takes little to find a willing partner. In order to help your understanding, I will tell you that this festival compares to the modern festival of Carnival in Brazil, which, of course, makes Mardi Gras look tame.

I make my way past the canals that intersect the city to the main road that leads to the Temple of Bast. The temple, built in a valley so all the city has a good view of the interior, is crowded with worshippers who make their sacrifices. Many in the crowd remark at the beauty of the building, saying that it is the loveliest red granite they have ever seen. I also hear voices filled with wonder speak of the tall trees within the temple, stating that nowhere else in the land does a temple contain a grove of trees.

A man sees me and attempts to pick me up, his intention being to carry me in his basket as is customary for cats in Bubastis, but I would rather explore on my own and scamper away.

As I pass one of the canals I notice a man squatting at the edge, relieving himself of his meal. As he finishes, he stumbles, apparently from having partaken of too much fermented drink, and falls into the canal. My, what a commotion. He sputters and wails and flails his arms as if the canal were as deep as the ocean. In fact, he could stand on the bottom without it covering his head.

His friends quickly come to his aid and assist him in getting out of the canal, but not without considerable grumbling, for the stench is putrid. While it is common for the canals to be used for human waste disposal, the number of festival goers doing so makes this accident extremely unfortunate.

I continue towards the center of the city and just past a large crowd of animated celebrants I notice a small group of men, somberly sitting around a table, playing Senet. While it has not always been so, tonight the game has taken on a magical meaning. The men have decided that the stakes are no less than the ability to pass through the netherworld upon death and achieve resurrection. I scurry away as I do not want to be nearby when the game ends.

As I make my way past the tombs where my fellow felines are mummified and buried, I get a chill. I know that someday soon, I, too, will pass on through this life.

It is late and I decide to find a place to sleep, providing I can do so with all the noise from the revelers. I approach the temple, which is now quiet. I make my way in and select a tree with a nice flat, low hanging branch on which I can rest.

In the morning I awaken at daybreak and make my way to the royal granaries to feast on the rodents that will undoubtedly be there. I pass many people sleeping—or laying in a state of unconsciousness. Most had the good sense to move out of the street and next to a building; most, but not all. Some are partially in the road and risk being trampled by merchants and farmers taking goods to market.

When I arrive at the granary, several women are already at work using wooden forks to separate the light chaff and straw from the grain. They smile at me as I stalk my prey and cheer when I make my kill. While I enjoy my feast, a few of the women use sieves made from reeds and palm leaves to separate the longer chaff and weeds from the grain. This work is very important to Egypt as what our people do not consume will be exported to other nations.

Yunet smiles at me and her smile melts my heart. I think she is the most beautiful woman in the land. Judging from the appreciative looks men give her, my opinion is shared by many. Yunet wipes the sweat from her brow and drinks water from the goatskin bladder before handing it to another woman and making her way to meet me. I purr loudly as she strokes my head and back and gently pulls my tail. She tells me I am a beautiful mau, and I nuzzle against her. If I would have a master, I would choose Yunet.

She sings to me in a voice so beautiful that, if I could, I would cry. I look up at her and she is crying. Her song is a goodbye song. She is telling me that she is leaving, going to a school for women in Sais where she will learn to become a doctor. I understand. She is always so compassionate; taking care of the sick must be her calling. I decide then that I will go with her.

I stay with her the remainder of the day and follow her to her home when the sun dips in the sky. Her family is excited to see me and decide that my presence is a great omen and a cause for celebration. Yunet helps in the preparation of the meal, consisting mainly of fresh vegetables with oil poured over, breads baked with honey, and beer made from the grain that Yunet has previously brought home. For this special occasion, the farewell dinner, her brother has purchased fish from the market. Her parents, two brothers, and sister share one fish. Yunet and I share the other.

They talk excitedly about Yunet's journey and the knowledge she will gain. Her medical skills will be in great demand upon her return, helping women through childbirth, an extremely dangerous and revered time in their lives.

"You will miss Kafele," her mother proclaims, referring to Yunet's betrothed.

Yunet sighs. "Yes, I will. We have spoken and agreed that this is what I should do. He is patient and generous and willing to wait for me. When I return, we will have a lavish wedding feast." She laughs and kisses her mother and sisters.

"How long will you be gone, Sister?" Anippe asks.

Yunet seems to ponder this before answering. "I'm not certain, Sister. I must study the texts and show that I have mastered their knowledge. I hope to return before the next flood waters."

The talk continues as the sisters enjoy eating figs and dates and planning their futures. I grow weary and make my way to the rooftop where it is cooler in the light desert breeze and I can look at the stars. It's been a long day. Tomorrow I will start my journey with Yunet. I must sleep.

***

"Come, Tumaini," Yunet beckons, using the name she has chosen for me. I remember the night she first bestowed the name. She was struggling with her studies and found comfort in my company. "I will call you Tumaini, — Hope—because that is what your presence gives to me. She held me a long time and showered me with kisses and I truly felt I was in paradise.

***

Yunet was excited and anxious to return to her home. Her schooling had taken nine cycles of the moon and now she would be able to perform duties as a midwife. I found the length of the schooling to be interesting, the same length as the human gestation period. Apparently Yunet had not realized this, or at least she had not mentioned it to me.

It was not an easy period for her. Oh, she did quite well in her studies; that was not the problem at all. It was her homesickness that almost caused her to fail. At times she would find it difficult to concentrate as her thoughts drifted to her family, wondering how they were, and dreaming of her return. She also missed Kafele tremendously and wondered if he would grow weary of her absence and find another to wed. He had already shown extreme patience with her, she reasoned. She was four years past the marrying age of her twelfth year, and most of her peers were already wed and starting families. "We will start a family soon after our marriage," Yunet told me one day as she brushed my fur. "How many children have you sired," she asked me with a rueful grin. Imagine. A gentleman never discusses such things.

One day there was a great commotion at the entrance to the school. A messenger had arrived with a note for Yunet. She accepted the papyrus scroll and gave the messenger a small piece of silver as payment. She brought the scroll to her room and read aloud to me.

"My dearest Yunet. I hope this finds you well. The number of days before you return are few. I miss you so much. Each day I pray to Bast to keep you safe and well and to return you to me soon. How is the mau? I hope he is well and is keeping your spirits up and the number of rodents down. I look forward to your return so that we can begin our life together. With all my love, Kafele."

She kissed the scroll, then kissed my head. "He misses us, Tumaini, and I miss him. It won't be long now before we can return home," she assured me.

The journey home would take five days. Yunet seemed to be trying to make it in four. I found it difficult at first to keep up, but as the sun rose higher in the sky, she wearied and the pace slowed. Occasionally we would stop to rest under the shade of a fig tree and nibble on its fruit. Yunet would share water from the goatskin bladder and, later that day, when we reached a village, she replenished the water from the community well.

Our first night was spent in a level branch of great tree near a place where two tongues of the mighty Nile branched out. Yunet made a bed from papyrus and used her bag of linen, which contained her clothing and copy of teachings, as a pillow. I wanted to stay on the ground near the river so that I could easily hunt and drink, but Yunet would have none of it. "Sometimes you hunt, Tumaini," she told me, "and sometimes you are hunted." She pointed to the reeds at the edge of the water where I could barely make out the snout and yellow eyes of a crocodile.

The next day our pace was slower and the day uneventful. Yunet was still anxious to get home but had resigned herself to the fact that she could not make the difficult journey any faster. We were crossing the delta of the great Nile from Sais to Bubastis; we would end up crossing water seven times before we were home. Each crossing required caution as snakes, crocodiles, and occasionally human predators needed to be considered.

Our second night was spent in the camp of some fishermen who eyed Yunet hopefully until she told them she was betrothed. They inquired as to why she journeyed alone and it perturbed me that, in their eyes, I didn't count. Yunet told them how she had gone to school at Sais to become a midwife and was now returning home. One of the men, Manu, told her of his sister Nubit, who lived in a village between Busiris and Leontopolis. "She is with child but she is poor and cannot afford a midwife. Please, would you go to her and help her deliver the baby?"

Yunet told him that she would go but that the timing of the birth of the child was unpredictable. "The baby may be already born when I arrive, or not ready to come into the world," she told him. "Still, I will stop and check on her."

Manu was very pleased and produced a nice perch that he allowed us to roast over the fire and eat. This was a great gesture on his part as the perch was his prize catch. The other fish in his basket were either carp or catfish. I believe that was the best meal I have ever had.

At daybreak Manu took us in his boat to the far bank and, after telling him goodbye, we resumed our journey. Yunet didn't speak much to me during this part of the journey; it was as if her mind was on other things. Perhaps seeing Kafele and her family again. Perhaps Nubit and the promise she had made to Manu to help deliver her child.

The sun was just past its high point in the sky when we entered the village that Manu had said his sister lived in. We stopped for water at the well and Yunet inquired as to where she might find Nubit. We didn't need an answer. The scream pierced the air like my fangs through a rat. "Come, Tumaini, we must hurry," Yunet urged me.

The labor and delivery were not easy and I feared the worst. Yunet worked with Nubit, following the teachings from her scrolls and soothing, comforting Nubit, wiping the sweat from her brow and the tears from her eyes. I sat in a window so that the slight breeze from outside carried the unpleasant odors away from me and filled my lungs with clean air. Nubit saw me and smiled through her tears; it nearly broke my heart.

"The baby is ready now," Yunet told Nubit, "but you are not. I will need to cut you so that the baby will be able come out. I will try to make the pain more bearable, but it will still be very painful. I need for you to be brave."

I couldn't watch and turned to look out the window. I said a prayer to the Creator that Nubit and the baby would survive, though my instincts told me they would not. I had heard the wailing before and knew that many babies died during childbirth, and that many mothers did, too.

The sun was low in the sky when I first heard the baby's cry. What a beautiful sound. I meowed loudly and Yunet turned to look at me and smiled. She held the baby in her hands, its cord still attached, and laid him on Nubit's stomach. She tied the cord and announced to Nubit, "It's a boy. A beautiful baby boy." Nubit did not answer. Her eyes were closed and I could not tell from my perch in the window if her chest was moving with the breath of life.

Yunet attended to the baby, cutting his cord and cleaning him before wrapping him in a blanket and handing him to Nubit's mother. Her attention turned to Nubit and it was then that I noticed the bed was covered in blood. I turned away and jumped out the window to the ground below.

Just after nightfall, Yunet came outside looking for me. "Tumaini, where are you?" she called and I tried to detect whether her voice contained sadness. I jumped down from a nearby tree and came to her. "There you are," she said in relief as she stroked my back and scratched behind my ears. "Are you hungry or have you already eaten?" She picked me up and carried me inside where the smell of fish cooking on fire wafted through the air and teased my nostrils. I licked my lips, flicked my tail and meowed. "I see," she laughed, "you are hungry."

She set me on the floor and immediately I decided to explore the home. It didn't take long as it was small and sparsely furnished. I avoided the room where Nubit had given birth, not certain what I would find there and unwilling to give in to my curiosity.

My attention was diverted by the sound of flesh splattering on the dirt floor near where I stood. Nubit's mother had dropped a fish head and one of the eyes had plopped out. I pounced on it and quickly took it into my mouth where it slipped over my tongue and into my jaws and squirted as I bit down into it. So tasty. I made quick work of the rest of the head, too, much to the amusement of the humans.

After dinner I sat in a corner cleaning myself when I heard the cry of the baby, followed by a reassuring voice. "There now, Nifé-en-Ankh, Breath of Life, I know you are hungry. Drink from my breast, my love." It was the voice of Nubit. She lives. I was so happy I jumped up and chased my tail in a circle seven times.

We slept on the roof of Nubit's home that night. Beneath the stars, I fell asleep as Yunet talked endlessly about the miracle of life and her experience helping Nubit with the birth of Nifé-en Ankh. "I'm going to like being a midwife Tumaini. I think it's what I was born to do," she said as she stroked me until I was fast asleep.

The next morning we continued our journey and once again Yunet resumed her quick pace. She was invigorated by the birth experience as well as excited about making it home. Her steps were quick and light and I struggled to keep the pace. Sometimes I would call to her and she would stop and come back to pick me up.

"What's the matter, Tumaini, you can't keep up?" she teased. "Here, I will carry you a while," she said as she held me in her arms. I enjoyed being held by her but knew that she couldn't do this for the entire journey. Eventually, I would wriggle free and jump to the ground, especially when there was something particularly interesting that caught my eye or my nose.

The family of Nubit had given us some figs and a bit of bread for our journey. We had stopped at the well and filled our goatskin bladder before starting out, and now that the sun was directly overhead, we stopped in the shade of a sycamore tree to eat and rest. Before I would let Yunet sit near the tree, I crept about it, looking for snakes or scorpions that might harm her. Satisfied that it was safe, I allowed her to sit at the base of the tree and rest against the trunk.

I scampered toward the water, which we were never far from, and soon found my own meal. I brought my prize back to show Yunet, who, to my dismay, was not pleased to see it.

"Tumaini, don't put that filthy rat on me," she shrieked as she jumped up to avoid having me place my bounty in her lap. I was insulted. Insulted, but hungry, so I took it out of her sight and feasted.

After my meal and a short nap, I heard Yunet preparing to leave. The sun was moving to the west and I could tell that, despite the heat, Yunet was anxious to continue our journey. Soon we were on our way, continuing the last leg of our return to Bubastis.

As we neared the city, someone recognized Yunet and ran to tell her family and Kafele of our arrival. A short distance inside the city gateway, the mother and sisters of Yunet came running towards us. They reached us, swarming around Yunet, hugging and kissing her with great affection and all chattering at the same time. Anippe took the load from Yunet while her mother draped an arm around Yunet and guided her toward home.

"We are so glad you are home, Yunet. We have missed you so much. Now you are finally here and soon there will be a wedding and a family," her mother says excitedly.

We turn a corner and suddenly Yunet cries out Kafele's name. He is coming down the street and, when he sees her, breaks into a run. I notice a slight movement near the wall of a pottery vendor who is desperately trying to get Yunet's attention, hoping to sell her "the finest painted pots the Greeks have produced."

I track the mouse with my eyes as it scampers along the wall. It sees me and immediately changes course. It attempts to run for cover, back along the wall toward the vendor. I spring toward it when abruptly I am hit and my breath immediately escapes me. I roll through the dirt and slam into a large pot. I lay there, trying to catch my breath, wondering what happened, when I hear Anippe shriek. I look up to see the stack of pottery, large and heavy, falling upon me. I cannot move and suddenly I see nothing.

My next recollection is not of sight but of sounds. I hear voices, many voices. They are angry and shout, "Cat killer, he must pay." I try to open my eyes, to move, but I cannot. Something is still pinning me to the ground. I can taste blood in my mouth.

"It is forbidden to kill a cat." I hear the priest say. "Bast will not be pleased. The law is clear, you must die."

"Please," Yunet begs. "Please do not do this. It was an accident. He did not see Tumaini, Tumaini came out of nowhere. He couldn't stop. Please, it could not be avoided."

"Enough," the priest commands. "Accident or not, the law is clear. Death by stoning."

The crowd cheers at this announcement and I can hear people moving about excitedly as they gather stones.

I am finally able to open my eyes and after a moment they find focus. My breathing is labored as I fight to swallow blood and breathe in air. I still cannot move, though I'm sure nothing is on top of me. It's as if my bones won't work, won't allow me to even twitch. I try to call out to Yunet, but the sound sticks in my throat.

I see the crowd now, gathered in a circle around someone in the middle. I catch glimpses of Anippe holding Yunet and both are crying. The priest stands at the inner edge of the crowd and holds a stone the size of his fist high above his head. "The will of Bast be done," he proclaims and the crowd repeats his words. He throws the stone with all his might and I hear a crack as it finds its mark on bone beneath flesh. I hear one shout of pain before the crowd begins the onslaught, heaving stone after stone until there are no more left to cast.

A great silence falls on the crowd as the priest goes to the accused. After checking the man, he announces, "It is done. Praise Bast."

The crowd cheers once more and slowly they dissipate, each going back to their own business, their own lives. In a moment only Anippe, Yunet, and their mother remain. They remove the stones from the deceased, wailing all the while. Yunet's brother arrives and helps her lift the man. It is Kafele. My heart is sick. What have they done? I am not dead. They have killed an innocent man. Poor Kafele. Poor Yunet. I do not wish to go on.

Life Two ~ The Battle for Jerusalem

Jerusalem
Late May-Mid July, 1099

The smoke from the surrounding farms billows in gusts toward the city on the cool spring air, making it difficult to breathe. Grim-faced men watch from the battlements on the city walls as everything in a fifty-mile radius of the city is aflame and more than one wipes the moisture from his eyes at the sight. I am certain that the tearing of their eyes is from the caustic effect of the smoke and not from any emotion at watching their homeland burn. These are battle-hardened soldiers who are practical and not given to tender-hearted thoughts.

This is the holy city of Jerusalem and we are preparing for war. Marching toward our city from Constantinople is the Christian army, Crusaders they have been named, with fifteen hundred knights and twelve thousand foot soldiers. I have heard this spoken of in hushed tones by the citizens of our city who insist they are not afraid, that our city is impregnable, that our defenses are formidable with walls fifty feet high and ten feet thick. I am only a simple cat, but I can sense their fear despite what they say.

I look at Commander Kahlid, upon whose shoulders rest the defense of the city and the safety of all that dwell within. Although uneasy, I am also reassured. He is a good man and an able leader. I know because I have lived with him and his daughter for the past four summers. I came to them from the Egyptian ruler, Al-Mustali Biallah, as a gift for the commander's daughter, Fatima, for her thirteenth birthday to celebrate her passage from girl-child to woman. Dimly, I can still recall being taken from my mother and placed into Fatima's outstretched arms. When the commander was given his new assignment in Jerusalem, I came with them. It is very different here, but I have come to regard it as my home.

My stomach rumbles and I lose interest in the soldiers' activities. Slowly I make my way to the house I share with Fatima and her father. The scent of roasting lamb reaches my nostrils and temporarily overpowers the stench of the smoke that travels through the city. I always like to watch as Fatima prepares the evening meal, and I settle myself comfortably on a nearby cushion to clean my fur as she busies herself basting the meat, chopping fruit, and steaming rice. She tosses me scraps of meat, which I daintily eat. Although not a great beauty, with wavy ebony hair that reaches below her waist and snapping black eyes that proclaim both a keen intelligence and lively wit, she is pleasant to watch. I also know that she has a kind heart. An only child, she is doted upon with obvious affection by her father; even more so since her mother died of fever two years ago.

I must have fallen asleep because it is with a start that I hear Kahlid's quiet footsteps as he enters. He pauses in the doorway and I notice how careworn he looks as he watches his daughter move between cooking pot and table, filling their trenchers with lamb, figs, sabra fruit, and rice. Sensing his presence, Fatima turns a radiant smile in his direction and runs to kiss his cheek.

"Father, you are weary," she says softly with concern. "I fear that you are working too hard. Come and sit."

"Yes, I am tired, but I am only doing what I must," he replies as he removes his outer robe and takes a seat at the table. He dips his fingers into a small bowl of rosemary scented water then dries them on the square of linen that lies next to it. Scooping the meat and rice mixture into his mouth with his fingers, he closes his eyes in appreciation of the taste. "Excellent, Fatima."

"Thank you, Father." She toys with her food then suddenly blurts out, "Is it really necessary to burn the farms?"

With a sigh, he nods. "Yes. It is also necessary to poison the wells outside the city walls. We are destroying everything." He rubs his hand over his eyes and then meets those of his daughter. "I do not like this either, but we have heard that the Christian army will be here soon after the next full moon." He notes her wide eyes and pushes his food around on his trencher as he considers his next words.

"Daughter, I will not lie to you. We are facing treacherous times. This Christian army is calling themselves holy Crusaders and think they are doing God's will by purging Jerusalem of the infidels and restoring it to the glory of God. They are nothing but murderers and rapists," he ends bitterly and spits upon the floor in his rage. Then he seems to gather himself and continues in a voice full of conviction.

"Jerusalem has been under Moslem rule for over four hundred and fifty years and it will not fall to these invaders. This I vow by all that is sacred to me. We will prevail. Allah is with us."

Her dark eyes full of fear, Fatima moves swiftly to her father's side and falls to her knees beside him. "Father, I do not understand. Is not their Creator also our Creator? God. Allah. Christian. Moslem. It is all the same. Why do they not know this?" Her lips tremble as she presses them firmly together and struggles to maintain her composure.

I see the anger drain from Kahlid entirely now, making him look just tired and worried. He sighs again and strokes her hair gently. "I do not know, my child. I fear that this holy war of theirs is driven more by ignorance and perhaps even greed than by faith. We must stand firm."

Laying her head upon his leg she whispers, "I know you will protect Jerusalem, Father. I know you will save us and our city."

Kahlid does not answer but continues stroking his daughter's hair with a faraway look on his face.

Disconcerted, I slip outside and head back toward the city gates, thinking of what I have heard, thinking of the approaching army, of the Crusaders who have decided it is their God-given duty to free Jerusalem from the *infidels*. Fatima's words come back to me. *God. Allah. Christian. Moslem. It is all the same.*

Alas, it seems not so.

The days pass one into another and still no sign of the Christian army. Perhaps they have given up and have returned to their homelands. At least this is what the people say to each other as they watch the horizon and dare to verbalize their hope. Most of the Christians in the city—yes, Christians from the East and Moslems have lived in harmony in Jerusalem for many, many years—leave for the safety of distant places. Commander Kahlid does nothing to discourage them as he prefers that only Moslems and Jews remain within the city walls for the coming battle. He says he does not want the Christians to have to make a choice, the wrong choice, between their faith and their city. I find Commander Kahlid praying more often than usual in the Mosque of Al-Aqsa or, as the Jews call it, Solomon's Temple. I have heard it said that the Ark of the Covenant, wrapped tightly in a veil of blue cloth to conceal it from all eyes, is buried deep in the ground within its sacred walls, but I do not know if this is fact or fiction. Regardless, it gives me little solace.

On a beautiful, sunlit day, the 7th of June, the Christian army appears suddenly and without warning. No trumpets sound their arrival, just an eerie silence broken only by the neighing of horses and the rumble of thousands of falling footsteps. The reports of the vastness of the army were not exaggerated, and I see a momentary flicker of fear in Commander Kahlid's eyes as he surveys it before he arranges his features into a mask of supreme confidence.

He turns to one of his captains and says almost too loudly, "Although the army is many, the walls of our city are strong and will withstand them. Praise be to Allah."

The captain agrees and they walk off together discussing the final details of the defense of the city. Curious, I climb a set of stairs that run upwards along the inside of the walls until I reach the top and can peer down at the enemy. The men are milling about setting up a campsite barely half a mile from us. They are raising their flags: one of two golden lions facing each other upon a background of sapphire, and the other of a white cross upon a background of crimson. The ground seems to tremble with the sheer number of them and, becoming agitated, I hiss at them. Hurriedly, I jump down and go in search of Fatima, much in need of comfort.

The next few days pass in a state of hushed expectation and strange peacefulness. The Crusaders seem to be in no hurry to attack us and set about making themselves comfortable and scouting the nearby land. This is a concern to Kahlid as he comes to the obvious realization that the enemy is not going to rush into battle and make careless mistakes. Instead, it seems that they will proceed with the "liberation" of the holy city with great deliberation. I overhear him discussing this with his war council and some suggest antagonizing the Christian army in the hope that their anger will make them careless. Commander Kahlid listens and then agrees to allow it.

The next day our soldiers line the tops of the walls and jeer at the men camped nearest to the city walls. Insults are traded and then a flurry of arrows is loosed upon our soldiers. Our men only laugh and break the arrows, then toss them back over the walls while asking each other loudly if perhaps some of the camp women are trying to get their attention by shooting Cupid's arrows at them. Several ribald jokes are passed back and forth. This goes on for quite some time until I hear shouts from our captains that the Christian army is indeed on the move. Thus begins a reckless attempt by the Crusaders to breach the walls of Jerusalem. It ends in failure and the Christian army retreats to its campsite in great disarray, with many dead and wounded, much to the delight of Commander Kahlid's men. I find a place near the wall and set about giving myself a bath as I listen to their self-congratulatory tales of the events of the past few days. Their excitement and pride is evident.

When the commander leaves to go home late that evening, I follow along. Fatima greets her father and begs him to tell her of the day's happenings.

"Father, I am so proud of you. The Christian army must surely leave and things will return to normal."

Kahlid rubs his hand over his eyes and shakes his head almost imperceptibly. "I fear, Daughter, that we may be rejoicing too much and too soon. I am well pleased with our men's success today, but their almost unbridled pride concerns me as well."

"But why, Father?" Fatima looks at him in bewilderment. "They have done a great thing. Why should they not be proud?"

"Because, my daughter. It is written that 'Pride goeth before a great fall' and I do not wish this to be the fate of our city. We must remain ever watchful and careful. I fear this is but a skirmish in a much larger war." He sits down heavily and gestures for a drink of spiced tea. Taking a long pull on the flask and wiping his mouth on his sleeve, he continues, "We must not underestimate our enemy. It would be our undoing."

A couple of weeks later a very strange thing happens. Suddenly, the entire Christian army begins to march barefoot around the walls of the city in solemn procession, praying and chanting. At first our soldiers watch them in disbelief, then begin once again to jeer at and mock them. The Christians ignore them this time and continue to circle the walls of the city three times before returning to their campsite. No one knows what to make of this behavior, but it has made everyone uneasy.

The next day we are stunned to learn that the Christians have somehow acquired a good deal of timber. *Was not everything burned?* They have set about building two siege towers. We are powerless to do anything to stop this as they are assembling them far from the reach of our fire-tipped arrows. Kahlid watches grimly, remarking to his captains that the true battle will soon be engaged.

Curiosity overcomes me once again and I long to sneak down into the enemy camp, as these strange men intrigue and repulse me in equal measure. I see my chance when I notice a loose stone at the base of one of the walls. Under cover of darkness I return to it and, with a bit of scratching and digging, I am able to pull it free. Now that the moon has risen, I see that there is nothing between me and the outside. The hole goes all the way through. Surprised and exhilarated, I crawl through and then creep along the ditch surrounding the walls until I am closer to the enemy encampment. Then I slink, with my belly near to the ground so I am not seen, until I reach where the horses are kept. They are tethered in a circle on the outer reaches of the camp and some snort and stamp their hooves at my approach, but the vast majority of them ignore me. I guess they have seen many cats in the stables in which they are normally housed.

Two men, one dark-haired and the other fair, both broad shouldered and powerfully built, approach the horses and stand only a few feet from me, staring at the city walls. I listen to them in shock as they talk about how the infidels living inside *their* holy city practice human sacrifice and idol worship. About how they eat the flesh of their dead and violate the laws of godly men. *How absurd.*

"Do you truly believe these claims," asks the dark-haired man of the other.

He shrugs and answers, "Does it really matter? We have taken an oath to return Jerusalem to Christian rule. That is all that matters." He grins and I can see the gleam of his teeth, white in the moonlight, as he continues, "Also, it is known that once Jerusalem has been taken, it will need a ruler and I can see no reason why that shall not be me."

Both men laugh and the talk turns to the plans for the battle that will begin as soon as the siege towers are completed. The towers will be draped with animal skins soaked with water to repel the flaming arrows that will certainly be fired upon them as they are moved toward the city walls. The assault will be a two-pronged attack, northwest and south, and once it is determined which side is the least defended, they will focus on that weakness. I shiver as I listen and begin to fear once again for my human family.

My movement must have caught the attention of the men because the next thing I know one of them snatches me up by the scruff of my neck. I hiss, twisting and turning, trying to get free, but to no avail. The man merely laughs and pushes me into the finely meshed chain-link hauberk that covers his chest and holds me there. A gloved hand strokes my head and I force myself to be still, although my heart is pounding as he does this. After a while I relax a bit as it appears that he means me no harm.

The clank of metal as sword strikes against light armor signals the approach of yet another man and he greets the two men respectfully by name, Godfrey of Bouillon and Robert, Duke of Normandy.

"Milords, your presence is required at the siege towers. They are near completed."

The dark-haired man holding me, Robert of Normandy, gives me a final pat and says as he places me on the ground, "A wise creature would not return to the city of Jerusalem as the battle will begin when the moon rises tomorrow night." Sounding pleased he adds, "We are ahead of schedule. The battle will begin in the pre-dawn hours of the 14th of July and within a couple of days, Jerusalem will be ours. Remember these dates. They will be marked in history as our time of glory."

Of course I run straight to the wall and make my way back inside the city. I will not abandon my humans.

The next day I watch with dread as the sun begins to sink and the enemy drapes the siege towers in the water-soaked skins discussed the night before. I know that they will then be moved into place along the walls as soon as the moon rises and I feel ill with trepidation of the battle to come. I find Fatima and spend most of the night curled up in her lap as she sits by the fireplace. Both of us spend a sleepless night. Commander Kahlid does not come home, but I am certain he also spends a sleepless night trying in vain to keep the siege towers from getting near to the city walls.

The new day dawns and I hear the battle cry of the Crusaders, "Dieu li volt!" *God wills it!* The battle begins in earnest. I am torn between remaining with Fatima and needing to see what is happening. Finally, I can stand it no more and leave her to run to the city walls.

Flaming arrows are being loosed and large stones heaved upon the enemy below as they try to raise scaling ladders to breach the walls. But slowly and ever so steadily the towers move closer, one to the northwest and one to the south, seemingly impervious to the stone missiles and fiery arrows. This time, as Commander Kahlid has predicted, they are better prepared as well as determined.

Men on both sides of the wall die. It appears that the Christians sustain more casualties than we, but this does not stop them. The fighting continues the entire day and into the evening, until an uneasy silence falls and both armies seek to rest and regroup. All know that this is but a temporary respite. The citizens are growing ever more fearful;

they have spent the day putting out fires started by the blazing arrows shot over the city walls by the enemy archers. The men are soot-covered and weary. Few words are spoken as they settle down to rest. A few minor skirmishes break out during the night between the two armies, but it is quiet for the most part.

The next morning, with the dew still wet upon the ground, the battle begins again. At mid-day a bridge is made from the siege tower to the south wall and simultaneously the scaling ladders are erected. Men begin to climb up the inside of the siege tower, protected from the flaming arrows by the water-soaked hides. They rush to reach the top where they will cross the bridge that stretches the short distance between tower and wall.

In a separate assault, the Christians begin to climb the scaling ladders. Boiling oil is pitched over the side of the wall onto them. The screams of the injured and dying echo throughout the city and I run away. Fatima steps into the courtyard of our home and stares in fear in the direction of the sound. I leap into her arms and bury my head in her hair. Trembling, she carries me back inside and bolts the door firmly shut.

Not long after, Commander Kahlid bangs on the door and rushes inside when Fatima flings it open. He tells her to hide, that the south wall is in danger of collapse and that the Christian army will likely soon breach it. I hear her audible intake of breath and feel the rapid thud of her heart as she absorbs his words.

"But Father," she begins, "what of you? What will—"

"Obey me, Daughter," he shouts. "Do not ask questions. There is no time." Then he hurries away, back to the battle; back to the beginning of the end for our people.

Sobbing, Fatima runs to the cellar beneath the floor and takes refuge there. In her haste, I am left behind. Frightened, I follow Kahlid, not knowing what else to do.

Chaos greets me.

The Crusaders are climbing over the south wall and are now locked in hand-to-hand combat with our soldiers. The screams of the dying and the scent of blood overwhelm me and I hide under a small porch, staring out in terror and disbelief. *How can this be happening?* Moslems and Jews run side by side past me to the Mosque of Al-Aqsa and take refuge in the sanctuary, hoping that the holy site will keep them safe. Men, women, and children huddle within its walls and I can hear them praying, beseeching Allah and Jehovah to save them, to not forsake them in their hour of need.

Some of the Crusaders fight their way to the gates of the city and after a fierce battle throw them open. I see Commander Kahlid pitched over the wall, numerous arrows in his chest and back, and I know that he is dead.

The killing of innocents begins. The Christians run into houses and drag out the occupants, killing them without mercy. Corpses are flung into the streets and men fall over them and each other in their haste to join the slaughter and take their vengeance upon the people. As the battle continues to rage, they begin to loot the homes and even the holy shrines for valuables and then set the torch to them. I have never seen such carnage. A Jewish synagogue is set on fire and the soldiers wait by the door to slay all who try to escape.

Men. Women. Children. It does not matter. They kill them all.

Some of the Christian commanders try to regain control but it is fruitless. Their men refuse to listen and continue their butchery, allowing no one to escape. I turn my eyes away as I see a mother and child cleaved in two by a huge battle axe wielded by a giant of a man who is screaming with excitement and blood lust.

I cannot stand it.

Bodies begin to pile one on top of another and my insides heave at the sight. Wails of terror and cries for mercy fill the air, at times almost drowning out the sounds of dying. Almost.

The streets begin to run red with blood and men appear to wade through it as it covers their ankles. Our home is approached by soldiers and I cry out but I am certain no one notices. I can hear them ransacking it and then they leave, carrying armloads of treasured valuables. *Did they find Fatima's hiding place?* I am too terrified to go and find out.

Approaching hoof beats draw my attention and I turn to see Godfrey of Bouillon rein in his huge white stallion. The horse's legs are covered in blood and gore and this splashes upon his boots and leggings as he struggles to control his mount. The stallion rears, its eyes rolling wildly as he urges it nearer to some of his men.

"Cease." His hoarse shout is ignored and the soldiers run onward. "By all the saints, you will rue this day."

He is now alongside some of them and strikes at them with the flat of his sword, yelling and cursing. I do not know what would have happened next because, with a final curse, he whirls his horse toward the Mosque of Al-Aqsa, a place that is said to be holy even to these Christians. It is said that they, too, believe the Ark of the Covenant is buried there and within it the Holy Grail. I track his path with dazed eyes and realize that he, along with Robert, Duke of Normandy, is trying to stop their men.

At first it appears they will succeed, then the doors of the temple give way and the Crusaders rush inside with swords drawn. Godfrey's stallion nearly goes down in the assault and it is a miracle that it regains its footing. The screams from inside the mosque tell me what is happening and I back up further into my hiding place, trying to block out the sounds. I lose sight of both Godfrey of Bouillon and Duke Robert as they are swept aside by those charging into the temple and others spilling forth from it, dead or dying.

Night falls and the killing continues. *Will it ever cease?* I fear not. Finally, near dawn, a deathly quiet falls over the city. Unsure of what I will find I crawl from my hiding place and go in search of Fatima. As I enter the house I see that the cellar doors are open, hanging at precarious angles. Silently I make my way down the cellar steps and there I find her. Her eyes stare sightlessly up at the ceiling. Protruding from her abdomen is the hilt of a knife. I recognize it as one of her father's and hope that the fatal wound was self-inflicted as I do not want her to have suffered. Numbed by all that has happened, I curl up next to her body. There I remain for two days and two nights.

On the third day, I make my way outside and, hearing the sounds of cheering, I stumble toward it. There, sitting upon his white stallion, is Godfrey of Bouillon. He is reading from a scroll to the assembled men. His voice carries to me as he tells them with obvious relief that by order of Pope Urban II they have all been given Papal Indulgence, which grants them immediate remission of all their sins, including the looting and burning of holy shrines. I realize this must be the reason that he and Duke Robert were trying to stop their men from entering the holy Mosque of Al-Aqsa, not to save lives but to avoid the displeasure of their Pope.

The reading of the scroll continues and it is now stated by order of the Pope that he, Godfrey of Bouillon, has been named Guardian of Jerusalem and will rule the city, thus returning it to Christianity as it had been when part of the Byzantine Empire. The Crusader army cheers yet again. I see Duke Robert, his arm in a sling, give Godfrey a slightly mocking salute with his uninjured hand and Godfrey smile back in return. All is as they said it would be a few moonlit nights ago.

The stench of decaying flesh mixes with the odor of burning corpses from the many funeral pyres throughout the city and I turn away, looking for a way to leave this place. Thirty thousand people of Jerusalem have died in this "holy war" and I cannot stay here with the victors. I suddenly remember the narrow hole in the wall that I used to visit the Crusader campsite and pick my way gingerly through the still gore-filled streets. Upon reaching the site, without a backwards glance I slip through the opening and run. I run and I run and I run until I can run no more. Everything is blackened and in ruins but after much searching I find shelter in an abandoned badger's den and fall into an exhausted sleep.

I will never return to Jerusalem.

Life Three ~ The Innocent Hammer

 I lay on the loft windowsill languorously washing myself, the gentle spring breeze from the open window drying me. Occasionally I stop, my ear twitching at the distant sound of a lark or a swallow. I hope upon hope that one will decide to leave the sanctuary of the woods for the promise of a nice meal within the confines of the barn, but so far ….

My attention is pulled toward the stall of Klaus, the Clydesdale whose job is to pull the wagon into the town the humans call Baden. He's stood, causing a mouse to scamper up the barn wall to the loft where I wait, famished. My eyes track its movements along the back of the barn, closer … closer. I pounce, claws extended and—dinner is served.

The barn door swings open and Alena shuffles in, huffing with the weight of child. "Dirk," she calls. "Dirk, are you in here?"

I creep silently toward a corner where I can enjoy my dinner in peace.

"Aaahhh," Alena screeches.

I freeze, certain she has seen me with my meal. I drop into a crouch, ready to make a quick exit.

She kneels over, clutching at her abdomen, and cries out again. Her brown hair is matted and I can see beads of sweat on her forehead.

"Alena," a distant voice calls. I hear running footsteps. There are two—no, wait, three men running toward the barn. I make sure my meal is ready for me to masticate, and slide it beneath the straw. Curiosity trumps hunger, pulling me to the edge of the loft where I can peer below.

"Alena," Dirk calls in alarm as he rushes to her side. "What is it?"

She looks at him, her hazel eyes large, betraying her fear. Her gaze falls to her lap and all eyes follow hers to the large dark stain spreading there.

Dirk sweeps her into his arms and lifts her. "Otto, you and Calvin go into town and bring back the midwife Gretchen. Hurry!"

Forgetting my hunger, I leap into the haystack below the loft and from there to the ground. I trot to the barn door and watch as Dirk carries Alena over the threshold through the wood frame door of the house, his arms strong from years of farming. I sense the pain and the danger. I must go to the house.

Turning my head I see Calvin and Otto disappear down the footpath from Mount Merkur toward the bridge that crosses the Oos, leading into town.

I run to the corner of the stone farmhouse, pressing my body against the smooth cool stones. I hear Alena's cries from within and Dirk's voice, trying to comfort her. Still, I can hear the distress in the timbre of his and I hope that Otto and Calvin return quickly with Gretchen.

Gretchen, sweet, kind Gretchen; she will know what to do. She always does.

I remember the first time I heard of her. She had come to Baden from Geneva just a few years earlier and had taken up residence with the family of the Markgraf as a caretaker for the children. The circumstances of how she came to travel alone, being an attractive young woman of marrying age, was the subject of much speculation in Baden. What was apparent and, therefore, not speculated on, was her intelligence. Still, many openly questioned the doctor when, during an outbreak of fever, he sought her counsel. Everyone knew that women were simply imperfect versions of men.

Soon the fever ceased and some in Baden felt that it was Gretchen who had saved the town. It was not long before some women, particularly those with child, sought her advice, which is how she became a midwife in Baden.

Despite her intelligence, or perhaps because of it, not everyone was enamored with Gretchen. Truth be told, some women, perhaps noticing the not-so-discrete glances their husbands cast toward her, complained to the clergy. Some even suggested, through vicious rumors, that Gretchen was bewitching the men of Baden. Indeed.

If men were bewitched, it was not the fault of Gretchen. She dressed modestly, usually in black, with no makeup, her honey hair in the style of the merchant class instead of the aristocracy with whom she lived. Always the lady, she behaved humbly and courteously. One could certainly not blame her for the fairness of her features, the fullness of her figure, the kindness of her smile, or the sparkle of intelligence in her eyes.

As time passed Gretchen successfully delivered a dozen new lives into the world, each time winning more acceptance in the community. So when Alena discovered that she was with child she was thrilled that Dirk, rebuking those who disparaged her, insisted Gretchen be employed as their midwife.

The first time Gretchen came to the house was a clear crisp autumn morning. Her breath made little puffs of white as she walked up the path from town. Her hair was pulled back and tied with a simple ribbon. She carried a canvas bag in one hand and a book in the other. A woman who could read, how unusual. In fact, other than nobility, few of the men outside the church could read. Certainly no women. This one, she must be special, I remember thinking.

Alena greeted her at the door and, after introductions, Gretchen entered the house, instructing Dirk to give them strict privacy. Retreating to the bedroom she closed the door, but not before I slid into the room.

"Is this your cat?" Gretchen asked Alena as she stared at me.

Alena shrugged her shoulders. "It lives in the barn with the other animals," she explained.

Gretchen set her bag at the foot of the bed and laid the book on top of the bag before approaching me. She knelt down and I moved against her, rubbing myself across the dress that covered her legs. She stroked me head to tail, then scratched behind my ears before picking me up. Turning toward Alena she asked, "Is it okay if the cat stays?"

Alena shrugged in indifference and sat on the bed.

Gretchen smiled at me and looked into my eyes, her own blue ones sparkling. "Okay, you can stay. But only if you behave and stay where I put you," she said, walking to the window and setting me on the sill.

"This is most unusual, is it not?" Alena asked. Noticing the puzzled look on Gretchen's face, she continued, "I mean, you coming here before the birthing time. That isn't what midwives normally do, is it?"

"No, I suppose not," Gretchen said. "I feel getting to know the woman with child and her condition throughout her term helps make the birthing easier. Are you agreeable to that?"

Alena looked out the window briefly before returning her gaze to Gretchen and nodding her head. "Yes, I am agreeable. I trust you."

Gretchen smiled and the warmth of it nearly melted me. "Thank you Alena, for trusting me. Trust is very important."

She returned to the foot of the bed, picked up the book and placed it on a small table. She opened the book and Alena gasped.

"Don't be alarmed," Gretchen said soothingly. "These are just pictures that will help me to know what is happening with your baby."

Alena glanced at the book as Gretchen flipped through the pages, drew in her breath with a start, and covered her mouth while looking away.

Gretchen looked up. "I'm sorry if you find these disturbing. They are drawings of the human body. For nearly a thousand years doctors have been using the descriptions provided by a man named Galen. Recently, a brilliant doctor named Vesalius decided that it was time to verify Galen's findings, so he studied the bodies of the dead.

"That's horrible," Alena shrieked.

Gretchen reached out and took one of Alena's hands in her own, rubbing her thumb across the top of Alena's to soothe her. "Perhaps a bit unsavory, but absolutely necessary. You see, there is so much we don't know about the human body and how it works. Without studying it, we cannot properly treat maladies. Too often treatments are based on religious beliefs, superstitions, or ill-conceived imaginings."

Alena frowned. "I'm not sure I understand you."

Gretchen smiled reassuringly. "I'm talking about knowledge. It's time we learn how things really are instead of guessing." She looked down at the book, which was open to a detailed picture of the human skeleton. "Do you know what Vesalius discovered about Galen's work?"

Alena looked wary and slowly shook her head.

"He learned that Galen's findings were based on the study of ape bodies. Apes instead of man, can you imagine? Similar, yes, but certainly different in significant ways. So for nearly a thousand years treatments have been based on apes instead of man."

Alena's expression became contemplative and after a moment she said, "That is truly horrible."

"Agreed," Gretchen replied, turning back to the book.

I was distracted by the flight of a lark whose shadow passed over me. I followed its path to its perch on the roof and, twisting my head, called out to it in the ancient voice all cats know to attract birds. Again and again I called, but without success. My attention was once again pulled back to the room by the sound of Gretchen closing the book.

"Everything seems fine," she told Alena as she reached for her bag. "I'll check in on you in a few months, and, please, send for me if you need me."

The women embraced and Alena showed Gretchen out.

***

Alena cries out above me and I know the baby is trying to come. In the distance I hear running and I know that Gretchen will soon be here. I crouch and spring upward, leaping to the open bedroom window. Perched on the sill, I survey the room and see Alena writhing on the bed, her face pale and sweat-covered, her hands clutching at the blanket. Dirk is stroking her hair, trying to soothe her through word and touch.

"Fetch a pail of water," I hear Gretchen say and I turn my head to see Otto running toward the well. "Build a fire," she instructs Calvin.

I hear the door open and footsteps navigating the house. Suddenly, Gretchen appears at the bedroom door. She moves quickly and without hesitation pulls Alena's dress above her waist. Moving her hands over Alena's midsection, she asks Dirk, "Do you have clean linens?"

"Yes."

"Fetch them, quickly."

"The fire is built," Calvin calls from outside the bedroom, "and Otto has the water."

"Pour it into the kettle over the fire. Tell me when it boils," Gretchen instructs from the bedroom.

She removes a waldglas jar from her bag and sets it on the table. Pulling the cork, she looks at Alena and says, "I'll make you a drink to lessen your discomfort."

The door swings open and Dirk enters carrying linens. "Place them there," Gretchen says pointing to a wood chair near the bed, "and fetch a stoneware mug."

Dirk frowns. I can tell he does not enjoy being given orders by a woman. But I see the fear in his eyes, the look of concern for his wife on his face. He leaves.

When he returns with the mug, Gretchen takes it from him and says, handing him the drinking jug, "When the water boils, fill this halfway."

Once he leaves, Gretchen moves quickly, removing Alena's clothing and covering her with clean linen. Using a small swatch, she reaches between Alena's legs. I turn away and when I look back the cloth, soaked through, lies on the floor near the bed. The smell of the blood of small animals has always excited me, but the scent of Alena's turns my stomach.

Between Alena's cries I hear voices and stirring in the front of the house and then Dirk is at the bedroom door. He gives the jug to Gretchen and moves to the side of his wife where he takes her hand and whispers assurances to her.

Gretchen peers into the mug that she has been swirling and nods. "Have her take this," she tells Dirk. "It will help ease her discomfort."

He looks warily at the contents, sniffs, then looks at Gretchen.

"It's an herbal tea that will help her relax." She nods reassuringly and Dirk helps Alena into a sitting position so she can drink. "Blow on it to cool it," Gretchen suggests.

She peers under the linen. "It's almost time," she announces.

When Alena finishes the potion, Gretchen asks Dirk to leave. He looks at his wife, who smiles her consent, and walks briskly from the room. Hearing the door close behind him, Gretchen pulls the linen back. "I need you to be strong, Alena. Your baby needs you to be strong. It is time for the birthing, but your baby is not in a good position. I will try to move your child but …."

Alena grunts, then cries out. Her breathing is fast, like she has been carrying a heavy load a long distance.

***

It has been what seems a long time with much thrashing and many cries, but now I hear a new one: the cry of a baby as it enters our world.

Gretchen places the child on her mother's stomach, and, reaching for the knife that she set near the bed, cuts the cord. She wipes the baby clean and wraps it before handing it to Alena. "It's a girl."

Alena smiles weakly, her eyes filling with tears as she takes her newborn into her arms for the first time. "Dirk," she calls and immediately the pacing outside the door ceases and he bursts through, moving to her side. There are kisses and embraces as the new parents are awash in the miracle of birth.

Gretchen puts the knife down and returns her attention to Alena, working to ensure she gets the afterbirth. Once that is accomplished, she places linen cloths in her patient's vaginal area, frowning at the amount of blood. She examines Alena, her fingers gently exploring tears in the flesh, a not entirely uncommon occurrence during birthing.

"Are you all right my love?" Dirk asks softly.

Alena does not reply. Gretchen looks at the woman, who is pale and barely able to keep her eyes open.

"Please, take the child," she says to Dirk. "Your wife needs rest."

Dirk looks confused as Gretchen places the baby in his arms and escorts him to the door. "Gently clean the child with water and clean linens. Then wrap her in a blanket and keep her near the fire so she stays warm. Not too close," she warns, raising her forefinger for emphasis. "Once Alena has rested I will call for you."

When Dirk departs, Gretchen places her ear against Alena's chest, her eyes watching the rise and fall of her breathing. Frowning, she checks Alena's eyes. Even I can see the pupils are abnormally large. She exhales, brow furrowed, and chews the inside of her cheek. Suddenly, she opens her bag and removes several long strips.

She moves quickly, placing the strips over Alena's tears. "These bandages should stop the bleeding," she says to me, though I believe she is trying to convince herself. In a matter of minutes, I realize it's in vain. The bleeding continues, not from the tears but from somewhere inside. There is nothing more she can do to help Alena. It's in God's hands now. All she can do is pray.

She slips from the room and I follow. She finds Dirk sitting on a stool near the hearth, holding his baby daughter, his face glowing with love. Otto and Calvin sit at a table nibbling slivers of cheese and drinking mead, their faces beaming as they celebrate their friend's good fortune.

Gretchen peers over Dirk's shoulder at the sleeping baby, so calm, so peaceful. She reaches her hand out to get his attention. But she hesitates, unwilling to interrupt the beauty of the moment. I hold my breath, knowing that what she is about to say will change Dirk's life forever.

Sensing her presence, he turns to her and smiles. She lowers her gaze.

"What is it?" he asks, his voice rife with concern, but quiet so as not to disturb his daughter.

Gretchen reaches for the baby, gently taking her from Dirk. She looks up at him, her eyes brimming with tears. "Go to your wife. Pray for a miracle."

Dirk's face immediately becomes ashen and he leaps to his feet. "Fetch the doctor," he calls out and moves quickly to the bedroom.

Otto and Calvin look at each other, exchange words in hushed tones, and it is Calvin who departs. Otto sits at the table, his gaze never leaving Gretchen. His expression betrays his suspicion and I fear what action he may take toward her.

Gretchen sits on the stool, gently rocking the baby, who had begun to stir. It occurs to me that Alena did not name the child. I wonder if she will ever be able to. Gretchen closes her eyes and begins to pray.

The house is dark with late afternoon shadows when Calvin returns with the doctor. He points toward the bedroom; the doctor gives Gretchen a contemptuous glare as he walks past her. Moments later, Dirk's cry confirms my worst fear.

Calvin and Otto exchange angry glances. When the doctor joins them, I fear for Gretchen's safety. They talk in whispers, one or the other occasionally looking toward Gretchen, who silently weeps, still holding the baby. When Dirk joins them, there is a brief discussion. It is Dirk who approaches Gretchen. "Give her to me," he tells her in an even voice.

She does so without protest. As he turns away she asks, "Who will care for her?"

Without looking at her, he replies, "My daughter's welfare is no longer your concern. Leave us."

I follow Gretchen as she leaves. She needs the comfort of an understanding heart. I will provide that.

***

It has been nearly a fortnight since that fateful day. Gretchen has done her best to continue to discharge her duties as the caretaker for the Markgraf's children, though at night she cries herself to sleep, often holding me close until she succumbs to exhaustion. In Baden, the townsfolk gossip about her, some openly questioning her motives, as if Alena's death was part of a plan. "Perhaps she wanted the baby," I heard the baker's wife speculate. "Or the father," suggested the daughter of the dressmaker.

Soon stories are spread about the midwife Gretchen and her practices. "She concocted a brew," says an old woman, "that killed the farmer's wife."

"A witches brew?" asks another.

The old woman nods her head solemnly.

The gossip spreads like fire and soon there are calls upon the clergy to arrest the witch.

I know the pastor to be an ambitious man and I fear his motives. He meets with the most influential members of the congregation and with the leaders of the Markgraf's army. Assured of their support, he calls on the Markgraf, demanding justice. I position myself out of sight, blending into the shadows of the castle walls so that I can listen.

The Markgraf sits at a long wood table in the main hall of the castle. He frowns at the pastor, who sits at the opposite end. "You can't seriously be suggesting that Gretchen is a witch, can you?" He gestures with a sweeping motion of his arm, the bright orange sleeve of his shirt flashing like a flame over his black vest.

"I'm suggesting there is ample cause for a trial."

"A trial? You mean one of those mockeries where guilt is assumed and all accusations accepted without question?"

"The people are afraid. Afraid that Satan's agent walks among us and that ... *you* are protecting her."

The Markgraf stares across the table and I sense for the first time a shift from steely determination to concern for self-preservation.

"What do you know of what the people think?"

The pastor smiles. "I attend to the needs of my congregation, hear their confessions, their hopes and their concerns. But if you still doubt my word," he reaches into his cloak and removes a rolled document, holding it out for a servant, "I have a petition."

"A petition?" the Markgraf asks, accepting the document from the servant. "A petition for what?"

"For you to arrest Gretchen and hold her for trial.

"And if I refuse this petition?"

The pastor shrugs with mock indifference. "I've heard they would seek an audience with the prince. Perhaps they could discuss the merits of his legal system. I'm certain he wouldn't be pleased to know that his Markgraf, the man he charged to protect the border region and ensure civil rule, has allowed it to become a mockery."

"How have I let it become a mockery?" the Markgraf demanded.

"By harboring a witch," replied the pastor. "Perhaps you are under her control? Perhaps she has seduced you—"

"Nonsense!" But already he is reading the petition, carefully scrutinizing the names. When he finally looks up, my fears are realized.

"So be it."

***

Gretchen stands in the corner of the courtroom, shackled at the wrists. Her clothing is dirty, her hair mussed from the week she spent in the prison without any means for proper hygiene. She is thinner, too, as I know she refused most of the insect-infested food she was offered. I know; I was there.

On the day that she was arrested, I followed. They marched her through the muddy rutted streets of town, shackled and guarded closely by men with swords. Their intent, I heard the pastor say, was to show the townspeople that she had been taken and also to intimidate and humiliate her in hopes of gaining a quick confession.

Gretchen, however, would not be intimidated. She held her head up as she was paraded through town. Many of the townspeople seemed afraid of her and most sheltered their children in fear of the witch's power. Gretchen's steady gaze met the few who were brave enough to taunt, and it unsettled them.

When at last they arrived back at the castle, she was taken to a cell in the dungeon. It was the smallest of spaces, with barely enough room to lie down in the straw that was piled in a corner. Damp and cold, it was without access to an outer wall or window from which to gain fresh air or natural light.

I was able to gain access through a ground level window by squeezing between the bars and leaping to the floor below, not a difficult task for a cat. However, avoiding the guards was a bit more challenging. With only the faintest of glows from the oil lantern at the base of the stairway, I meandered through the dark, dank recesses of the jail, avoiding the outstretched hands of the other prisoners as I sought Gretchen.

Occasionally, I brushed against a wall that was slick with green slime and it disgusted me. I would definitely need to clean myself once I found Gretchen. Using my sense of smell, I soon slipped into her cell where I curled myself into a ball on her lap.

She reached down with a trembling hand and stroked my fur. "Thank you," she whispered. "Thank you for not forsaking me." I purred my affection and she leaned down and kissed my head. I could feel her body relax as she held me. Eventually, the rise and fall of her breathing became rhythmic, like a boat on a gently rolling sea, and sleep found us.

I awoke with a start at a noise emanating in the opposite corner. I saw two, then two more beady eyes peering at us. Rats. They'd come in search of the food scraps left on the floor of the cell by the jailer and I have no doubt that if they couldn't find sufficient quantities, would have turned their attention to Gretchen. Not on my watch.

I moved into a crouch, careful so that my movements would not attract their attention. When their heads bent to consume stale breadcrumbs, I leapt. Their shrieks ended abruptly as I crushed the windpipe of one with my jaws and slashed the jugular of the other with a fatal swipe of my claws.

Proud of my accomplishment, I brought one of the carcasses to Gretchen, who, surprisingly, refused my offer. "Take that filthy vermin away from me," she said flicking her hand. While I would have preferred to have feasted on my prey, I instead removed the carcasses from our cell out of deference to her. Dropping the rats on the floor, I heard the guard approaching. I quickly returned to the cell and hid in the straw behind Gretchen.

The guard stopped outside the cell, prodded the dead rats with the toe of his boot, and asked, "Witch, what have you done?"

"I'm not a witch," Gretchen called out to the guard who was hastily departing. "And I have done nothing wrong." It was the last time I heard her speak for three days.

And so we stayed together in the cell, comforting and protecting each other. I killed several more rats and only once succumbed to my hunger, though I did so outside the cell so as not to offend Gretchen.

While we shared physical proximately, we did not seem to share an emotional intimacy. Our physical contact was sparse and I worried that I wasn't being the comforting soul she needed. It was as if she had left this world and traveled to another and I wasn't sure if this was due to anger or fear. It was with some relief that, on the fourth day, she began to speak to me.

"It won't be long now," she said in an even voice. "The zealots will have sufficiently fanned the flames of fear and they will come for me."

I moved against her and she picked me up, cradling me to her chest and resting her chin gently on my head. "How quickly life changes," she sighed. "A few days ago I was in charge of the household of the Markgraf. Now I'm a captive in his prison below." She laughed and the sound of it was bitter as vinegar.

I shook my head, causing a tickle in her nose, and she smiled and kissed my head. "Thank you," she told me and I was surprised by her words. "You are the only one who has not abandoned me."

I reach out, gently touching her cheek with the pad of my paw.

She smiled and stroked my head. "All I ever wanted was to help people, to be like my father." Her words are soft and wistful. "He was the best doctor in the kingdom, the personal doctor of the Royal Family." She cleared her throat. "Knowledge, that's what made him so good. He didn't just accept ancient teachings, he tried to confirm them. When he couldn't, he met with other doctors and read accounts of their discoveries; men such as Pare, Vesalius, and Fracastoroa, who sought the truth through knowledge instead of giving in to superstitions."

She fell silent for a long while and it wasn't until I felt teardrops on my head that I understood her pain.

In the coming days she would tell me more about her life and how a good portion of it had been spent in the Royal Court. She recounted being with her father and learning from him as he tended to the sick and infirmed. Sometimes she would tell me stories from the books she had read. She predicted with excitement that someday books would be available to everyone. She was happy when she talked of her father—except for once. It was the story of her engagement.

"When I was the age of fifteen, I was introduced to the cousin of the prince. He was nineteen years old and physically not unattractive. He immediately let it be known that he intended to court me. I was flattered, to be sure, and at first it was wonderful. He would bring me gifts and sing songs to me while the royal musicians played. I was the envy of the 'ladies in waiting.'"

I meowed and she looked at me quizzically. "Am I boring you?"

I pushed my head against her hand and she stroked me head to tail. When she stopped after a half dozen times, I settled into her lap and nuzzled against her.

She continued, "Eventually I was told that I could no longer accompany my father when he cared for the ill. I was also to stop reading books as these pursuits were not considered *ladylike*. Instead, I was informed that I would be trained on important things such as proper dancing, planning parties, and managing servants. *Important?* How could anyone consider such trivial matters important? So I decided I couldn't continue the courtship. What I didn't understand was the consequences of my decision."

At this point her story was interrupted by the sound of an approaching guard. He peered into the cell before sliding a plate of mush under the door. He started to turn away when he stopped and looked back. Apparently my presence inspired a religious moment as the guard called out to God and made the sign of the cross before scurrying off.

For some reason I couldn't fathom, this interruption made her sad and her reminiscences ceased. She would not continue until the following day.

"I haven't seen my father for four years," she said as she watched me remove and devour the bugs from the day's mush. I stopped and looked at her. "When I told him of my intentions, he asked me why, and when I explained my reasons, he understood. But Father is a wise man and he warned me that the Royal Family might not take my decision well. He told me to expect some sort of punishment or humiliation, but neither of us expected the extent of their wrath."

At this point, hunger overtook her and she reached for the mush, scooped it with her fingers, and pushed it into her mouth. She devoured the meager offering in less than a minute and then sat back against the wall as the food settled in her stomach. I moved next to her and rubbed my face against her hand until she stroked my head. She looked down at me and smiled, though it was a smile full of heartache. "You are a good listener, friend. So where did we leave off?"

I meowed and she said, "That's right, the Royal wrath. When my father first presented my decision, they were incredulous. Deciding it was a matter of nerves, they pressed me to continue the relationship and, above all else, not to mention my decision to anyone.

"For a month I continued to see him and was civil but not affectionate. I certainly did not want to hurt his pride, but I had no intention of marrying him and did not want him getting false hopes to the contrary. I told him those very words but to no avail. I informed him that I would not be attending the Royal Christmas Ball, but he did not believe me—at first.

"They sent a carriage for me and I refused to go. I was not in proper attire, so forcing me to go would have caused them embarrassment. There was some confusion and angry discussion as to what to do when, finally, the guard in charge informed me that I was being taken into custody. So, you see, this is not the first time I have been placed in a cell."

I crawled onto her lap and she hugged me. "They pressured my father to force me to marry but he would not and offered his resignation. Eventually, they decided to banish me from the kingdom. I was fortunate that the Markgraf, who knew and respected my father, was in need of a caretaker for his children. He arranged for me to come to Baden."

The sound of footsteps descending the stairs ended her story. Soon there were three guards outside the cell. "Stand, witch," one commanded.

"I'm not a witch," Gretchen insisted, but stood.

They entered the cell, shackled her wrists, and pulled her roughly out the door. "Bring the familiar," the one in charge commanded, and before I could react I was snatched by the scruff of my neck and shoved into a bag.

Now Gretchen stands trial and I watch from the cage they have placed me in. The courtroom is packed, and the crowd, boisterous until this point, falls silent as the charges are read.

The judge asks who will be stating the case against the accused and the pastor steps forward. An excited murmur goes through the crowd and the judge barks, "Begin."

The pastor recounts a quick history of Gretchen's arrival in Baden and the subsequent outbreak of fever, insinuating that she was the cause. He follows that with the complaints he received that Gretchen had been bewitching the men of Baden and had others attest to that fact. At last he got to the day that Alena died during childbirth. After providing a scathing summary where he accused her of poisoning Alena, he had the doctor recount the strange bindings he found on Alena when he examined her body. Otto and Calvin told the court how Gretchen often referred to a book of spells containing drawings of men and women, their bodies naked and mutilated. Excited whispers follow this testimony and when I looked at Gretchen, she sadly shook her head slowly side to side.

Finally, the pastor brought in the jailor who told of the dead rats outside Gretchen's cell and how she had summoned her cat, an agent of Satan, to her cell. All eyes turned to me and I shrank to the corner as best I could.

"Her cat," the pastor bellowed, "was also present when she attended to Alena, the farmer's wife. I suspect the evil creature was instrumental in helping her carry out her depravity."

"Kill the witch," someone called from the gallery.

"And the cat," said another.

"Enough," Gretchen screamed and silence fell over the room. "I am not a witch and the cat is simply a barn cat. One who, like me, is curious as to how the world works. He has befriended me when all others have forsaken me. Even those of you I have helped."

My ears picked up the nervous murmurs scattered about the room as Gretchen continued.

"The book you referred to is a book of knowledge, compiled from the best doctors from the great sea to the south to the mighty kingdoms in the north. The drawings are depictions of wounds treated on the battlefield as well as the study of human remains. This knowledge," her voice now rose above the chattering of the crowd, "is allowing better treatment of the sick and wounded. It is time we end practices based on superstitions and embrace the pursuit of knowledge."

The pastor glanced around the room before shouting, "Silence, witch." He looked at the judge and continued, "She is using her powers to confuse our minds. Beelzebub himself may be speaking through her."

"How dare you," Gretchen shrieked. "How dare you tell these lies? You know I am not a witch and that Satan has no power over us."

A collective gasp in the courtroom and a smile played at the corner of the pastor's mouth.

"So you refute the findings of the Church?"

"What findings? The findings of the early believers that demons were no more than tempting nuisances, not capable of great harm?"

"The findings of the Hammer," the pastor said, and, noticing the crowd seemed more confused than convinced, continued, "Nearly a hundred years ago Pope Innocent VIII authorized two monks, Sprenger and Kramer, to investigate whether demons and witches existed. They concluded that not only did they exist, but also they existed in vast numbers, capable of horrible wickedness. Their report, *The Hammer*, provided us with a system to determine who was a witch and how they should be dealt with."

"Lies and superstition," Gretchen challenged.

"Many witches have been caught and most have confessed their crimes. They have often talked of others who walk among us. One boldly claimed that the number of witches was in the tens of thousands."

At this revelation, many in the courtroom grew fearful and some again called for the death of the witch and her cat. "Burn them. Burn them at the stake."

When the judge did not act to silence them, more took up the call.

I turned to look at Gretchen, expecting her to fight back, but this time she was silent. She shook her head, tears spilling down her cheeks, as the crowd grew louder and angrier. "I am not a witch," I heard her say, "and

I forgive you."

Once again the crowd took up their cry for killing the witch and a few pelted us with rotten vegetables. The judge ordered us back to the jail while preparations could be made for our execution.

In the damp darkness of the jail I cry out for Gretchen. I long to sit in her lap and comfort her, but they have placed me in an adjoining cell and left me caged. I cry out time and again until I hear her sweet gentle voice.

"There, there my little friend, there is no use crying. Our time has come and soon we will die. I'm sorry that your life, your precious innocent life, will be taken, but crying will not change things. Take comfort that soon this will be over and perhaps we will go to a better place. Maybe to the Creator's home where we will sit at his table. Imagine that, my friend. Imagine a place without pain and suffering, a place where everyone and everything is good. Imagine that place and take comfort that soon we will be there."

Her words are comforting and I focus on them until, in the darkness, my eyes grow heavy and I start to sleep.

I am startled by the sound of footsteps on the stairs and I can see shadows on the wall from the glow of a lamp. Six armed men stand before Gretchen's cell. "It is time, Witch," the one in charge says and they enter her cell and pull her to her feet.

Next they come for me and roughly snatch up my cage by the handle on top. As we near the top of the stairs I hear excited murmurs. We step into the courtyard and it seems as if most of the town is here. When they see us they cheer, eager for the entertainment of our death. "Like Christians being taken to the lions," I hear Gretchen say.

The closer we get, the more frenzied the crowd, a mob, really, becomes. I recognize some of the people, people who I had known to be kind and compassionate. But they have changed into something evil. They lust for death and shout insults at us. Some spit on us while others, still fearful of our supposed powers, shrink away when we come near.

The crowd has gathered around something I cannot yet see. As we approach, they part, allowing us passage. They are ten deep and when we are halfway through I see the stake. It is large, probably seven feet high and two in circumference. Piles of dried brush and small branches lie nearby and I cry out in fear as I realize what this means.

They are rough when they bound Gretchen to the stake, showing no regard for her as a woman or even a person. Ropes around her head, shoulders, waist, and feet prevent her from any movement. They set my cage next to her and my only vantage point is a view of the contorted, vile faces of the mob.

The jeers and calls for our death crescendo as the brush and branches are placed around us but end abruptly when the pastor steps forward from the crowd. He speaks about evil and how it must be stopped at all costs. His voice rising, he proclaims us agents of Satan, stating those in concert with the devil present a danger to the world and must be eradicated. When he ends, the Markgraf steps forward.

"In accordance with our law, the convicted are granted last words."

A gasp is heard from some in the crowd who shout out protests. "She'll cast a spell," cry some while others declare, "she'll summon Satan."

Ignoring them, the Markgraf turns to Gretchen and asks if she has any last words.

When Gretchen speaks I am certain she is looking directly at the pastor. "I am not a witch and this cat is not an agent of Satan. My crime is being a woman and seeking knowledge, knowledge which I used for good, to help people. And this cat, it killed the rodents that ate your grain and brought disease among you. And it, too, sought knowledge, always curious about the wonders of God's world. Yet you condemn *us to* death. You claim *we* are evil. But I say it is *you* who are corrupt and evil. I do not fear death as I know I will soon join my maker in paradise." She pauses for just a second before adding, "But I fear for you. My God has a special place in hell for those who harm others in his name. That blasphemy will not be forgiven. May God have mercy on your souls."

Life Four ~ Victoria's Song

Gazing at myself in the mirror, which I must admit is one of my favorite pastimes, I brushed away a silky strand of hair that was tickling my nose. Soft green eyes stared back at me as I perused my reflection for several more minutes. Finally growing bored, although I *was* looking at perfection, I rose and stretched languorously, then sighed with contentment. Most unusual for December, the sun streamed warmth through the open window, and the light breeze that filtered through the curtains drew me toward it with a gentle siren's song. Reaching the window, I batted aside one of the curtains and pushed my head and neck through the opening to feel the warmth upon them. I closed my eyes, enjoying this rare respite from the dreary cold of winter.

Suddenly, my lovely tranquility was broken by guttural barks and howls in the alley below. Annoyed, I opened my eyes and looked downward, focusing on the two ruffians making the god-awful racket. Two mutts, obviously of unknown parentage, were playing a raucous game of tag, taking turns chasing each other back and forth through the narrow alley. *Dogs! I detested them.*

With deliberate slowness I reached out and touched the potted plant sitting on the window sill … tap, tap, tap. Three times I lightly tapped the plant. Then, as soon as the dogs were directly beneath my window, I shoved the plant with all my might, sending it into the air where it hung suspended for a fraction of a second before hurtling to earth. The startled yelps from below filled me with satisfaction.

"What have you done?"

I turned at the loud voice and pushed quickly away from the window, striving without success to achieve a look of innocence. I was feeling much too smug for that.

The housekeeper, Mrs. Trunbalt, clucked her tongue in dismay as she leaned out the window and saw the ruined aloe plant amid the shattered pottery and scattered soil.

"You have been very naughty," she said as she turned to glare at me.

Unrepentant, I shrugged, but moved further away from her just in case she decided to follow up her scolding with a smack or slap. Rarely did she raise her voice to me, much less strike me, but I *had* just shoved one of her precious aloe plants out the window so I didn't think I should allow her to get too close.

Soft footsteps followed by an even softer voice drew my attention and I sidled toward the sound.

"What is wrong?"

Mrs. Trunbalt drew herself up to her full height of less than five feet and dramatically pointed a finger in my direction. "That *creature* destroyed the aloe plant. Deliberately. I saw her do it."

Victoria Graham, a slender young girl with dark blonde hair and azure blue eyes, turned toward me with a look of dismay on her pretty face.

"Belle, come here at once," she said sternly, cocking her head in my direction.

Silently, and somewhat sheepishly, I padded toward her, knowing that she was able to track my progress even though she could not see me. When I reached her she knelt down and swept me up into her arms and, as always, I snuggled against her and began to purr.

"I am sorry about the plant. I will ask Papa to replace it." I could see that the sweet earnestness with which she spoke melted the anger in the older woman.

Mrs. Trunbalt sighed. "Do not worry about it, Miss Victoria. We have others as they are very useful to treat ailments of the skin. It's a blessing for it to be so warm this time of year and I thought the sun would be good for them. I didn't think any harm would come, but your cat pushed it out the window. She is a bad one, she is." With that, she huffed a final time to mark her displeasure with me and left the room.

"You should not do such bad things, Belle," Victoria admonished. "Did the dogs in the alley upset you again? You really must learn to ignore them." She ruffled my soft white fur with a delicate hand and gave me a quick hug.

"I must practice now," she said, placing me on the bed. I settled myself comfortably and patiently waited for her to begin. With swift, sure steps she crossed the room and sat on the bench before the dark, glossy piano.

Victoria's maternal grandmother had left the beautiful—and expensive—piano to her when she was only five, which was the same year I came to live in this household. Family members, most of them aged and without youthful dreams or aspiration, voiced their opinion that it was a strange bequest to a blind child, but Victoria's father had stated with confidence that his daughter could do anything she put her mind to, regardless of any physical limitations.

She had proven him right.

Touching the keys lightly yet confidently, Victoria began to play. Entranced, I listened to the delightful melody and watched the girl as she lost herself in the music. This was the highlight of my day. Well, with the exception of looking at myself in the mirror.

After a time the music stopped and I yawned, having been lulled into drowsiness. Victoria smiled and turned toward me, glowing with happiness as she always did after a practice session.

"Tomorrow is Christmas Day, Belle. Papa says he is bringing me a special present to celebrate my 'ascent into womanhood' when he returns from Paris tonight. You'd think I was of a marriageable age, for goodness sake." She blushed and giggled as she apparently found that thought very amusing.

I blinked and made no comment, although I realized that being a girl in one's thirteenth year was a special year indeed. It made her almost all grown up.

I also must admit that I very much enjoyed the Christmas celebration each year. Victoria had explained to me in great detail about the Christ child and the tradition of gift giving as she had prettily wrapped a present for her father. Her gift to me had been a lovely pink ribbon with a tiny silver bell sewn on it. She'd placed it about my neck and it had tinkled merrily when I moved about. I had looked quite pretty.

Christmas was always a festive and joyous time in the Graham household. I particularly looked forward to the feast that would be prepared as I was always given a large dish of honeyed sweet cream and a portion of roast goose. I licked my lips in anticipation.

"I am going down to supper now, Belle. Please do not get into any more mischief." Humming happily to herself she left me. I flicked my tail lazily and cocked an ear toward the open window. Not hearing the wretched dogs in the alleyway I decided to remain where I was and take a nap.

***

The next morning dawned raw and cold with no hint of the warmth of the day before. The dismal weather did nothing to dispel the sunny disposition of my youthful companion. That's how I thought of Victoria: she was my companion as I was hers. Sometimes people said that she owned me, but we both knew better than that. I was an independent spirit and, as much as I loved Victoria, she would never own me.

Victoria slipped into her robe and slippers and hurried from the room. I could hear the slight brushing sound made by her fingertips as she lightly ran them along the hallway wall as she skipped along it.

"Papa," she sang out as she reached the closed door to her father's bedroom and rapped quickly upon it. "It's Christmas morning. Come, let us celebrate." She knocked again. "Papa?" Then more softly, "Papa, are you awake?"

I heard heavier footsteps as Mrs. Trunbalt came up the stairs onto the second floor. "Your father has not come yet, Miss Victoria."

"Oh. But he was due back last night. He promised he would be here for Christmas." Disappointment tinged her voice.

"I know, Miss. Something must have delayed him, but I'm certain he'll be here soon. He's always been a man of his word, he has."

"Of course he will be here soon." Victoria echoed. "I will wait to have breakfast until he arrives."

"But the food is ready and it will grow cold."

"Then we will warm it up. Papa and I always have breakfast together on Christmas morning. You may eat, but I will wait."

I peeked around the corner into the hall and saw the stubborn set to Victoria's jaw, a rare sight indeed, and knew that she would get her way in this. Mrs. Trunbalt bobbed her head in compliance.

By late morning the clouds had nearly departed and the sun appeared, although it did nothing to warm the day and the cold wind still held the promise of snow. Winter had returned.

To celebrate Christmas Day the citizens paraded noisily through the streets, calling to those watching on the sidelines or from their windows. Laughter and singing along with shouts of "Good Christmas to you" filled the air as I sat next to Victoria on a bench placed by the front window. She waved half-heartedly when the carolers paused before our house and sang a merry Christmas tune.

By mid-afternoon snow began to fall and Victoria's father not yet arrived, nor was there any word as to why he was delayed. I lay on

Victoria's lap to keep her company as she sat waiting by the fire in the parlor. The girl's stomach gurgled and growled, but she refused to eat, drinking only a cup of tea in the morning and that at the insistence of Mrs. Trunbalt.

The Christmas feast that had been prepared was now served and eaten, but it was a solemn affair without the usual lightness and gaiety. I lapped my honeyed sweet cream and ate my slice of roast goose, enjoying them, I must admit, although less than usual. The gingerbread cake, made especially for Victoria's father, as it was his favorite, was untouched and would remain so by tacit agreement until he arrived to partake of it.

The evening hours passed slowly and the snow continued to fall, blanketing the streets with a soft white carpet that glistened under the street lamps. Victoria paced, becoming more agitated each time the clock on the fireplace mantle chimed, marking another hour that had passed.

"Papa, where are you," she whispered, nearly in despair. I patted the hem of her dress and meowed softly to try to comfort her. She looked down and I could see tears shimmering in her eyes. "Oh, Belle. I'm so worried that something terrible has happened. He would be here if he could. He has never missed Christmas with me. Never. Oh, what has happened?"

My sweet Victoria, don't worry. It will be all right. I knew she couldn't hear me, but was certain she could feel my thoughts and take solace from them.

The house remained silent and a few hours later Mrs. Trunbalt banked the embers in the fireplaces and began to close up for the night. Without protest, Victoria allowed herself to be led upstairs and put to bed. I curled up next to her and placed my paw upon her cheek, finding it once again wet with tears.

Much later I heard the clock downstairs chime. Twelve times it pealed. Midnight. The witching hour, I've heard it called. A shiver ran down my spine and I huddled closer to Victoria, seeking my own consolation in her warmth. She tossed and turned and murmured fitfully in her sleep.

I kept watch over her until dawn.

***

The muffled clatter of hooves on snow covered cobblestones brought me to my feet. I ran downstairs to one of the windows at the front of the house to see what I could see. A tall man, travel-stained yet well dressed, dismounted from his horse. He paused a moment to retrieve a package, a gift perhaps, from a bag hanging on the side of his saddle then strode toward the front door. As he passed before me I could see that it wasn't Victoria's father and disappointment filled me, followed swiftly by trepidation. The man's face was lined and his mouth was set in a grim straight line. Instinctively I knew what he brought wasn't good and I wished him to go away.

Ears flattened against my head, I backed away from the window and headed toward the stairs, knowing that I had to reach Victoria before this dreadful man did.

I heard a loud knock upon the door and the murmur of voices as Mrs. Trunbalt greeted the visitor. A shriek of horror made me pause and look back at the entranceway. I saw the man catch Mrs. Trunbalt as she staggered back, reeling as though from a physical blow. His eyes were kind and sympathetic as he looked at me over the woman's head, but I didn't see him, I saw only Death standing there in the doorway.

I turned and fled up the stairs.

Arthur Graham, aged forty-two, had been taken with a sudden fever on his way home from a business trip to Paris. He died in the early morning hours of December 24th, 1732.

For the next few days, friends and acquaintances arrived and departed much like a somber carrousel, save there were no bright colors on this merry-go-round, only shades of gray and black. Much of the time Victoria remained in her room, gently holding an ornate music box, her father's Christmas gift to her. She wept and wept until I thought there could be no more tears left in the world.

Few relatives remained and only two of them, Victoria's Aunt Gladys and Uncle Roland Smithson, Arthur's younger sister and her husband, were willing to travel to attend to the funeral. I'd never heard of a funeral before, didn't know what one was, but I can tell you they are horrid and sad and that I wish never to see another.

A fortnight later the time had come to think about a permanent arrangement for Victoria. Arthur Graham hadn't been a rich man and, according to Gladys and Roland, there was little money to support his daughter. I lay on Victoria's lap and listened as they discussed the situation and made plans for her future. Neither of them thought to include the girl or to ask her opinion or wishes.

I liked them not.

They made it quite clear that Victoria would do as they said and be grateful they weren't putting her out on the street. No one really wanted her, a blind girl with little money and no prospect for a bridegroom in the future. Who would want to marry her? She would only be a burden to a husband, unable to care for him and any children of the union. My heart ached as I listened to these greedy, callous people talk in front of Victoria like she wasn't even there.

She's blind, you idiots, not deaf.

It was decided by Gladys and Roland that they would take Victoria's beautiful piano to cover the expense of the funeral for which they had supposedly paid. The house was quickly sold, for very little profit to hear them tell it, and arrangements made for Victoria to be sent to a home for those unable to care for themselves: McGregor's Home and Sanctuary.

Victoria would be well cared for as long as the money lasted, but that wouldn't be too long gauging by the speculative looks that passed between Gladys and Roland. As for me, there would be no room for a cat at the home so I would be left to fend for myself.

"Nasty beasties, cats are. I have no idea why Arthur put up with having one in his home," Gladys sniffed as she stared down her nose at me then swatted at me with the back of her hand. "The parlor is no place for the likes of you. Get out of here."

I hissed and stood my ground.

Victoria blinked and seemed to come awake after a long sleep. "Don't touch Belle. Leave her alone."

"Don't take that tone with me, little missy," Gladys said sharply. "I'll have that mangy cat thrown to the dogs, see if I don't," she added with a menacing look at me.

Victoria stood and gathered me in her arms. I could feel her shaking but her voice was strong and sure. "You won't touch Belle. I will not allow you to harm her." And together we left the room.

I heard Gladys say loudly, so that we could hear, "A lack of good manners and a lack of respect for her betters, that's what she's got. I don't know why Arthur coddled that girl so much. She'll soon be taken down a peg or two, though, Little Miss High-and-Mighty. And her foul cat will be eating garbage scraps." Their laughter followed us up the stairs.

Alas, they were true to their word.

***

The next few years were hard ones. Although I couldn't stay in the home with Victoria, she was able to sneak me a portion of her food each day and at night I slept in an abandoned house only a couple of streets away. But Victoria's stay at the home was short lived. The money from her father's meager estate, including the sale of the house, was gone all too soon.

"'Twill be debtor's prison for ye," said Mrs. McGregor, when the Smithsons neglected to send the monthly fee for Victoria's board for the second month in a row. "Ye can't stay here without paying yer rent, lassie."

I was hidden under Victoria's bed and so heard all that transpired. "But I may know of somewhere ye can go. Mrs. Varney owns the boarding house over on Hamilton Street and she be needin' a laundress. She won't pay ye much but ye won't be starvin'. And ye'll be able to pay me the two months' rent ye owe me. Of course, if ye'll give me that pretty music box of yers, I will call that an even exchange." Victoria shook her head and said she could never agree to part with the music box. It was all she had left of her father.

We left the next day. Mrs. Varney said she didn't mind a cat around as long as it earned its keep by killing the mice in the house. At least I'd be allowed to stay in Victoria's tiny room under the stairs.

From dawn 'til dusk Victoria washed the linens and clothing that Mrs. Varney gave her each morning. The old woman was surprised that nary a stain was missed, even though Victoria was sightless. I could have told her that it was because Victoria scrubbed them until her hands were raw from the hot water and harsh soap. It broke my heart that her once soft, delicate hands were now reddened and calloused.

How I longed for the days when I lounged before the mirror and my only concern was my reflection and getting even with the dogs in the alley. How long ago all of that seemed. I was getting older now and not as spry as in the flower of youth, but Victoria had only grown more beautiful in spite of her work-roughened hands.

Mrs. Varney seemed at times to have grown quite fond of Victoria and, yes, even of me. One evening when Victoria had just turned eighteen the woman asked Victoria to join her for supper. At the table was a young man who Mrs. Varney introduced as her nephew, Charles Lawson. The meal passed quite pleasantly and ended with Mr. Lawson appearing smitten with Victoria. He even kissed her hand and asked if he could see her the next evening.

"Y-yes," stammered Victoria, her cheeks flushing prettily. I watched with interest. Soon, whenever Charles Lawson was in town he came to see Victoria and even sent her letters when he was away. I thought good fortune had finally shone upon us.

I was wrong.

It turned out that Charles Lawson didn't want Victoria to be his wife. Oh, heavens no, a blind wife simply wouldn't do. But a blind mistress … that would be fine indeed.

On a warm summer's night Mr. Lawson made his proposal to Victoria. The sound of the resounding slap across his face marked the end of our tenure at Mrs. Varney's boarding house. The old woman was incensed that Victoria thought herself to be above the advances of a fine man like her nephew.

I wanted to scratch his eyes out.

Now we were truly on our own. I could feel Victoria's fear at being alone in a sighted world, but I also knew her determination.

"Belle, they are not going to break me. I'm going to be strong and make Papa proud of me."

We walked away from the boarding house with Mrs. Varney's last words ringing in our ears: "You'll be back in no time and we'll see if my nephew is good enough for you then. If he'll still have you, that is.

I took Victoria to the abandoned house where I had lived while she was at McGregor's and there she put her belongings. She'd brought enough bread and cheese to last us for a few days, but after that we had to go to the market and buy some food. A few people we met while walking jeered at us and said unkind things, some offered to help us find our way, but most of them simply ignored us.

"Belle, we haven't much money left," Victoria told me as we were going to the market a few weeks later. But her words didn't register with me. I heard something that made my heart lighter than it had been in a very long time.

Music.

Not just music but *music*. Someone was playing a piano and it sounded so beautiful that I couldn't resist going toward it. I tugged at Victoria's skirt and pulled her in that direction.

"What is it, Belle? Where are you taking me?"

Then I saw her cock her head to one side and I knew that she heard it, too.

"Oh," she said softly. "It's beautiful." Her feet began to move and we followed the sound of the music until we reached its source: an open window high above our heads. Without a thought I leapt upon a wooden beam and began to climb.

"Belle, no."

I could hear Victoria but chose to ignore her. I was curious and we all know what happens to a curious cat. No, not that. This curious cat found her sweet Victoria's beloved. Oh, yes. I found the man who would love Victoria the way she was meant to be loved.

His name was Andrew. Andrew Barstow.

When Andrew saw me on the window ledge peering in at him as he played the piano, he stopped and came over to me. He leaned out the window and looked down. Standing below in the alleyway was a beautiful young woman with dark golden hair shining in the sunlight dancing upon it.

He smiled and called down to her, asking if I were her cat and she responded in a way that immediately intrigued him.

"No, Belle isn't my cat. She's my companion. My friend."

I felt my heart swell with pride at her words.

"Perhaps then I should bring your friend down to you," he said laughingly. "Unless you'd rather leave her up here with me."

"Sir, if you don't mind, I'd rather leave her up there for now."

"Really? Why would you leave her here?"

"Because I would ask that you continue playing your song. It was so beautiful that I long to hear the rest of it." The wistfulness in her voice was enough to make me weep.

Andrew looked at her for a long moment then said, "Of course. I haven't finished writing it yet, though." He grinned and added a bit bashfully, "I'm a carpenter by trade but a composer at heart."

"You truly have a gift then, because it is wonderful."

He beamed down at her. Victoria couldn't see him, but I certainly could.

"Would you come up and listen?"

Victoria shook her head. "It would be unseemly to be in a gentleman's room without a proper chaperone."

Andrew nodded, "But of course you are right. There is a wooden box there for you to sit upon while I play."

"Please tell me exactly where it is, sir." She hesitated then took a deep breath and continued, "I cannot see it for I am blind."

I saw the startled look on the man's face be quickly followed by one of compassion as he directed her to the makeshift seat. And then he returned to the piano and began to play.

Victoria and Andrew were married within the month. Andrew became known in England as a composer of good renown. He didn't have worldwide acclaim, nor did he appear to wish it. He was happy and content to compose his music with his beautiful wife by his side, a wife who oftentimes played his music to rapt audiences who applauded her skill and beauty and did not call her blindness a disability. Andrew Barstow called himself a very lucky man.

And the song that he composed on the afternoon he met his future wife and her friend the cat? Well, he called it "Victoria's Song," although I really think he should have named it "Belle's Song." After all, I was the one who brought them together in the first place.

But truly I am quite content. I have food in my belly, a warm fire to curl up beside when it is cold, and my own mirror in which to gaze upon my reflection for as long as I like each day.

Hearing a noise I trot across the room and leap upon the sill of the open window and look down.

With deliberate slowness I reach out and touch the potted lily plant sitting on the window sill … tap, tap, tap. Three times I lightly tap the plant. Then as soon as they are directly beneath my window I shove the plant with all my might, sending it into the air where it hands suspended for a fraction of a second before hurtling to earth.

Satisfaction fills me at the startled yelps from below.

Dogs. I still detest them.

Life Five ~ The Ghost Dance

Dakota Territory
December 29, 1890

I thought it would never end. The shouting, the screaming, the crying, all punctuated by the sound of gunfire echoing near and far. Sometimes it was the deep booming blast of a heavy shotgun, but more often the lighter, sharper report of rifles, too many to count. And then, oh, horrors, the nearly continuous thunder of heavy artillery, of four Hotchkiss cannons, as I had heard them called, able to fire fifty rounds of nearly three-pound shells per minute. I saw all of the people I knew falling and then laying still against the snow. Never had I heard such dreadful sounds. I prayed that it would stop. Then it did, but perhaps that was even worse.

I lay hunched against the tree, a large old oak, too afraid to move. The thick haze of gunpowder settled over my surroundings, obscuring my vision of anything more than just a few feet away. It all happened so quickly that it's still difficult for my mind to process it all. My eyes burned and teared up from the smoke and the terrible things I have witnessed. I blinked furiously to clear them.

I heard them before I saw them. The sharp sound of their horses' shod hooves striking rock sent a shiver of fear up my spine and I felt the hair rise along my body in response to their growing nearness. Pushing myself more tightly against the tree I could only hope they would pass by without noticing me, but, to my alarm, they stopped just a couple of yards from where I was hiding.

There were two of them. They sat astride their mounts in their blue uniforms, surveying the area in a slow, meticulous manner. One of them gestured in my direction and the other nodded, urging his horse closer. He then dismounted and approached me with outstretched hands, mumbling unintelligible words in what I guess he thought was a soothing tone. Realizing that my only hope of avoiding capture was to climb the tree as quickly as possible and hope to attain a branch out of their reach, I leapt from my hiding place and began scaling upward. Adrenaline surged through my body and I moved impossibly fast. For a moment I thought I would be successful, then I felt a pair of hands pulling me roughly from the tree trunk.

I heard a cry of despair and realized with a shock that it was mine. Unwilling to be taken without a fight, I lashed out at my captor, but he was much larger and stronger than me. Deftly he pushed my limbs against my body and held them there firmly as he enfolded me in a blanket until only my head remained uncovered. With a few flicks of his wrist he skillfully tucked in the corners of the blanket until I was swaddled like a newborn baby and then lowered to the ground. I struggled furiously for several minutes until forced by sheer exhaustion to stop. So there I lay, helpless, my sides panting from exertion while I glared at him. He stared back at me without expression.

Gathering me in his arms, my captor carried me the short distance to where the other man sat waiting upon his huge bay stallion. The horse snorted and rolled its eyes, the whites standing out in sharp relief against its dark reddish brown coat. I was unceremoniously dumped into its rider's arms. The man gave a grunt of satisfaction as he gave me a cursory inspection and concluded that I was securely restrained. Without further ado I was draped across the front of the saddle, half resting upon the man's legs. With a cluck of his tongue and a nudge of his heels he urged his mount forward into a trot. Knowing it was futile to struggle further, I accepted my fate and squeezed my eyes tightly shut as I bounced along in rhythm with the horse's gait.

After what seemed an eternity we stopped. Grateful for the cessation of the bone-jarring movement I opened my eyes and surveyed my surroundings. I wished I hadn't.

Death was everywhere. The cold, gusting wind now carried large flakes of swirling snow that didn't fall fast enough to conceal the horror beneath their whiteness. No, not nearly fast enough. I heard myself utter a mewling whimper of grief and my captor reached down and gently stroked my cheek with calloused fingertips. I repaid his unwanted kindness by sinking my teeth into the flesh between his index finger and thumb. He swore and swiftly withdrew his hand, but did not retaliate.

His companion gave an unexpected snort of laughter. "Feisty little thing." The man holding me remained silent, so he continued, "Tell me, Sarge, why you wanna bother with some mangy cat?"

Sergeant Reginald Armstrong sighed tiredly. "There has been too much killing this day, Corporal Phelps. I think this poor creature is worthy of rescue."

I thought I detected a tremor in the one called Armstrong's voice and glanced over at him with curiosity. To my surprise I could see the glimmer of unshed tears in his eyes. I have seen soldiers in their blue uniforms and thought it unusual for the man to be affected in this manner. Turning my head what little I could, I brought the one named Phelps into my line of vision. He appeared to be ill at ease with this small display of emotion. The easy camaraderie that I had felt between the two men earlier vanished. Finally he cleared his throat and asked, "Are you all right, sir?"

"Look at what was done here this day. Why did it come to this?"

"We put down an Indian uprising, sir." The man sounded a little perplexed by the question. "Some of us may even get medals."

Surveying the hundreds of bodies of men, women, and children that were beginning to be covered by the fast-falling snow, Armstrong shook his head and said sadly, "No, I think not. There is no glory in what has happened here today at Wounded Knee Creek." The sergeant bowed his head and murmured so softly that Phelps had to strain to hear his words.

"May God have mercy on our souls."

***

I was born to the Parker family of South Dakota, a small gray and white in a litter of six others, in the spring of 1888. One of my first recollections was of feeling my way blindly around the cozy area the human family had created for my mother and her family. When I was finally able to open my eyes I was astonished by the sheer wonder of everything. I played and slept through many idyllic weeks, nurtured by my mother and kept company by my brothers and sisters. Some days the little girl who lived in the cabin, several yards from the barn in which I lived, would come and play with us. Her name was Emily Parker and she was sweet and gentle with us. Not so her two brothers, Johnny and Adam. They often played with us too roughly, causing their mother to reprimand them for their insensitive behavior. I quickly learned to avoid the two boys.

One day as I was dozing in the warm sun, I saw Emily approaching. With her was another young girl, one I had never seen before. Whereas Emily was fair skinned with pale reddish blonde hair and blue eyes, her companion was dusky skinned with deep brown eyes and black hair pulled into two long braids. Emily called her Falling Rain, which I thought was a very nice name. The two girls played with me for a time, scratching my ears and rubbing my belly, which I liked a great deal.

One day as Falling Rain was leaving, Emily kissed the top of my head and solemnly handed me to the girl. I snuggled comfortably into her arms and purred contentedly. That was the last time I saw Emily Parker, my mother, and siblings. Falling Rain's family had been relocated to the Pine Ridge Indian Reservation about fifty miles to the west and I was going with them. I was now a permanent part of her family, the Miniconjou Sioux; the Lakota people I heard them called.

We settled near the White Clay Creek that summer and the days were spent in getting used to our new home. The camp dogs loved to chase me until one day I turned upon my tormenters and fought back. I probably would've died that day due to my foolishness but the holy man of our tribe, Kicking Bird, came to my rescue. Shaking his stick, he proclaimed me a very important creature who fell under his protection and laid an elaborate curse upon any person or animal that dared to harm me. He then picked me up and carried me to Falling Rain and, to my amazement, as he handed me to her, I saw him wink conspiratorially at her. The corners of her mouth turned up in a brief smile which she hid by rubbing her face into my fur.

"Thank you, Uncle."

He responded by tugging on one of her braids lightly, then continued on his way. The camp dogs didn't bother me after that day. Everyone saw to that.

The winter was harsh and we suffered. The chief of our people, Big Foot, was a peaceful man and brought our many concerns regarding lack of material to make warm clothing and not enough food in a respectful manner to the Indian Agent assigned to us. The man made promises that were never kept. The Sioux were a proud race and it made the young men angry and bitter to see their chief groveling like a woman. They voiced their frustration and called for action, but cooler, wiser heads prevailed.

Everyone ate only one meal a day and did so sparingly for fear that the food would run out entirely. Falling Rain always shared her food with me. Since I was such a small animal, I didn't require much in order to survive. The ill and the elderly began to die and Chief Big Foot again approached the white man responsible for his people's well being for help. None was given, although once again promises were made. Finally the winter gave way to spring and although we didn't get the supplies that were guaranteed, the warmer weather gave them hope. At the end of April several wagons arrived and everyone rejoiced.

I was a year old now and no longer a kitten. Oh, I still liked to run and play, but I found myself spending more time among the people observing their ways. Most of them spent their time planting seeds in the earth, hoping for a bountiful crop come autumn. The children played and the adults watched them with smiles that are tinged with sadness. I listened to them speak amongst themselves and learned that much has been taken from them and how they yearn to return to the days when both they and the buffalo they hunted freely roamed the plains. It broke my heart to understand what had befallen them.

Summer came and, under the relentlessly blazing sun, the crops that were planted with such hope in the spring withered and died. The hope of the Miniconjou Sioux died with them. I was there when Chief Big Foot looked at his people and knew that he must do something to bring them back from their despondency. If not, he said, he feared they would all perish. He said he had heard of a Paiute holy man named Wovoka who resided in western Nevada and was the leader of a new doctrine of religion. Wovoka had been telling of a vision he'd had during an eclipse of the sun in which he had seen an apocalypse. The earth was destroyed and then recreated with the Indian people as the new inheritors of it. During this apocalypse the white man would be destroyed, the buffalo would return, and it would be a day of great rejoicing as the red man reclaimed his rightful place. I sat beside Kicking Bird as he listened to Chief Big Foot speak of the new belief called the Ghost Dance religion and I felt his uneasiness.

"We will send a delegation to Nevada to meet with Wovoka," the chief decreed.

Kicking Bird started to protest but Big Foot held up his hand for silence. "Our people need to have something to believe in. They have no faith in the white man and I fear they will soon have no faith in me." He surveyed the small group of men before him. "We must do this."

The men murmured among themselves and began to nod in agreement. Kicking Bird finally agreed as well, but did so with an obvious mixture of trepidation and yearning. Fear and hope rode side by side.

I followed him to his tent and lay down beside him hoping to ease his anxiety. Stroking my head absentmindedly, he told me of his concerns, wondering aloud if the Ghost Dance religion would be something to unite his people or if it would bring catastrophe to them all. He bowed his head and asked the Great Spirit for guidance. I fell asleep listening to the comforting rumble of his deep voice murmuring softly in prayer. When I awoke he was not there and I could see that his pallet had not been slept upon. I could only hope that he had found the answer he sought. He was a good man and I disliked seeing him troubled.

A band of ten men left two days later. Falling Rain's father, Running Deer, had insisted upon accompanying his brother-in-law on the trek. It would be a journey fraught with danger and he refused to let Kicking Bird go without him. They were gone for several weeks; it was the end of autumn when they finally returned. Chief Big Foot met them eagerly and ushered them into his tent to tell him of their meeting, to tell him of the Ghost Dance.

I watched as Screeching Hawk handed the chief the sacred garb that had been given them. They were bulletproof, according to the Indian messiah, Wovoka, and would protect them from the white man. Big Foot was clearly very pleased and said that a Ghost Dance would be held the next night to celebrate the safe return of their warriors. He instructed Kicking Bird, as holy man, to oversee the ceremony.

The next night the people all gathered and many of the men and some of the women attired themselves in beautiful garments for the dance. The women wore dresses of white, with bright colors about the neck, decorated throughout with moons and stars, birds, and animals. The men wore shirts and leggings in vivid shades of red and blue. The shirts also had vivid colors at the neck and were covered with bows and arrows in addition to the moons and stars and birds and animals on the dresses of the women. Some men painted their faces with these same symbols and some adorned themselves with feathers. I settled myself nearby and watched in fascination.

As the crowd gathered around Kicking Bird, he began his address, giving them directions as to the chant. After he had spoken for a while, he motioned for them to form a circle, standing behind each other, hands on the shoulders of the one before them. They circled a few times, chanting, "Father, I come," then they stopped and looked expectantly at Kicking Bird. He nodded and they began wailing, calling out the names of their dead friends and loved ones. As they called to the departed some took up handfuls of dust and threw it above them; others merely let the dirt and dust fall from their fingers back onto the ground. Finally, they raised their eyes to the sky and entreated the power of the Great Spirit to allow them to speak with those who had passed from this life. They began to circle again, faster and faster, until it appeared they would spin out of control, all the while entreating these ghosts to come forth and help them vanquish their enemies.

The wind from the dancers enveloped them in dust and sometimes even hid them from my view. Now the rest of the people joined, even the weak and the ill, as it had been foretold that the dance could cure them and this faith carried them forward on limbs suddenly powerful and strong. All chanted the words with great reverence as they circled with abandon:

Father, I come;
Mother, I come;
Brother, I come;
Father, give us back our arrows.

They repeated them over and over, louder and louder. Some dancers began to stagger away from the circle and fell to their knees while others pitched forward and lay motionless in the swirling dust. Others began pawing at the air, pulling at their hair then throwing their arms about wildly and shrieking. I thought it a wonder no one was trampled in the chaos.

Suddenly there was silence.

As the dust settled I could see that people were either lying unconscious or sitting dazed upon the ground. No one remained standing. I looked for Kicking Bird and saw him sitting not far away, staring at nothing, as if in a trance. Finally he touched a hand to his forehead and rose to his feet. Others began stirring as well.

I shook the dust from my fur and hurried away.

The dance had disturbed me.

***

The people seemed to find great solace in the dance and it was held during each full moon. As winter came again and conditions deteriorated once more, the frequency of the Ghost Dances increased. In the spring of 1890 the ceremonies were being held several times between the monthly cycles of the moon and it was causing great concern among the white settlers. They complained to the authorities and soon the Indian people were told to stop dancing. I again sat inside the tent of Chief Big Foot and listened as he explained the situation to the members of his council. Many expressed outrage at the continued interference of the white man into their personal lives. Even Kicking Bird, who had been against the Ghost Dance at first, was opposed to stopping it, stating that it brought comfort to the people. They had little and he was not willing to see this taken away. The vote was unanimous: they would not end the Ghost Dance ceremonies. The people of the Lakota were on a path of destruction that even I, as a simple cat, could see. I feared for my people.

In August, Chief Big Foot called another council meeting. As usual I slipped inside and took my place beside Kicking Bird. He didn't seem to notice my presence. There was great tension in the air and I dreaded to hear the cause. The chief spoke slowly and solemnly. The U.S. government, fearful that the Ghost Dance was actually a war dance, had issued an official order that it was to cease immediately.

Once again the council defiantly voted to allow the dance to continue. They would not be forced to renounce their new religion, one that gave them some small hope for the future. Besides, why should they relinquish everything to the white man? He had lied to them and not kept his promises. Why should they obey an order from such a people? They would not.

I looked at the angry faces of the men and shivered.

The next two months passed in a stalemate. The people of the Lakota continued to celebrate the Ghost Dance, sometimes as often as once a day, and the government insisted that it come to an end. A confrontation was inevitable.

Then in November we heard that troops were being sent to occupy the Lakota camps at Pine Ridge and Rosemont. The news was met with much muttering and the young men prepared to defend their right to continue the ceremonies. Chief Big Foot spoke out against resistance and told the young men to put down their weapons, to not be fools.

Once the troops were in place, the Ghost Dance ceremonies were not held as often as before, but it was impossible to keep the people from dancing. I saw the soldiers look on in fear and misunderstanding as they watched the ceremonies and I could feel the underlying, barely contained violence that I feared would soon erupt unless something was done. Apprehensive, I sought out Falling Rain more often than usual and found a little comfort in her arms as she held me and stroked my fur. I could see the same wary nervousness reflected in her eyes that I knew was in my own.

I was roused on a cold day in December by the sound of people packing their belongings. Not understanding what was happening, I stepped out into the pre-dawn light and watched in amazement as hundreds of people gathered their possessions and left the camp. I ran to Falling Rain and cried at her. She knelt beside me for a moment, running her hands along my back, then returned to placing her things inside a small knapsack. When she finished she went to her mother, Shining Dove, and together they walked toward the rest of the people. I heard someone say that it was a hundred and fifty miles to the east, through the badlands, to reach the camp of Red Cloud, another Sioux Chief. There, it was said, we would find food and shelter for all and would be able to celebrate the Ghost Dance without interference.

Confused and more than a little frightened, I hurried to catch up with Falling Rain. She smiled down at me as I trotted alongside her, obviously pleased that I was coming along. I soon wished I hadn't.

Five days later the blue-coated soldiers stopped us. We had only traveled about thirty miles from Pine Ridge. The slow progress was due to the illness of Big Foot, who had to ride in a wagon, and the number of women and children slowing the pace. I heard Running Deer say with apprehension that the Seventh Calvary had detained us. He insisted that they hated all Indians because of what had happened to General Custer at Little Big Horn. Shining Dove protested that the battle at Little Big Horn had happened nearly fifteen years earlier.

"No matter," Running Deer said with certainty. "See the cannons they have with them? Why do they have them? I tell you, they still hate us and would like to see all of us dead."

I was chilled by his words.

We were marched to Wounded Knee Creek and set up a makeshift camp there. Kicking Bird reported that there were about five hundred soldiers escorting us and I could tell that he was worried. He said he had heard that we were being relocated to a reservation in the Oklahoma territory in which the conditions were even worse than the dismal ones at Pine Ridge. No one knew if what Kicking Bird had heard was true, but if it was, it would be a death sentence for many. I leapt into Falling Rain's arms and rubbed my cheek against hers in an attempt to console her. She buried her face in my fur and I could feel her tears as she cried softly. I didn't know what else to do so I did nothing.

The next morning, December 29th, the soldiers went to Chief Big Foot and demanded that he turn over any guns that were in our camp. I had never realized how old the chief was until I saw him standing outside his tent attempting to reason with the soldiers, his shoulders hunched and shaking with illness and fatigue. After the soldiers left him and began to search each tent, determined to find any and all weapons that might be hidden within, he sank down on the ground and had to be carried back inside. I feared that his illness was mortal; I could hear him wheezing and gasping for breath.

To give the people hope, and perhaps also in defiance, Kicking Bird began the Ghost Dance chant. Several of the people, Running Deer included, removed their outer clothing to reveal Ghost Dance shirts beneath them and began to dance. One of the soldiers shouted at them to stop but was ignored.

I'm not sure what happened next, but I saw a soldier approach Black Coyote, who was deaf, and demand the old shotgun that he held. Probably not understanding what he wanted, Black Coyote pulled away from the soldier and accidentally discharged the shotgun. What happened next will forever be burned in my memory. Shots rang out and I watched in shock as suddenly men, both red and white, were running in all directions. The coppery scent of blood filled my nostrils. My first thought was for Falling Rain.

Frantically, I searched for her, but there was too much confusion, too many people, and too much dying. I could only hope that she had made her way to safety, if there was such a place in this hellish nightmare.

Terrified, I ran.

***

Now I was being held by one of those who had slaughtered my people. I tried to hate him, but I could feel his anguish. As I listened to his words, I realized that this man abhorred what had happened and that it grieved him. No, try as I might, I could not count this man as my enemy. Nor could I accept him as my friend. My heart was shattered as we rode away from the site of the massacre and I yowled, voicing my sorrow. The sound echoed eerily through the white swirling snow. From the edge of the forest I saw the spirit of Falling Rain sadly waving to me and I knew that I would soon die. I felt a sense of peace come over me, replacing my earlier fear.

Bury me at Wounded Knee, I thought, for that is where my heart lies.

Life Six ~ The Holy Man

 All is quiet, except for the soft snoring of the master in the upper room, yet I cannot find peace. My mind will not quiet; something strange is happening within me, like a million needles coursing through my blood. Silently I rise and move about the dwelling, checking the doors, the windows, and the remaining rooms, but all is quiet. Still, I cannot shake the feeling that something is about to happen. Something monumental. Something dreadful.

Unable to find danger and unable to sleep, I let my mind wander back to the beginning of our time together. I was barely a year in this life, feral some would say, belonging to no one, roaming the streets of the village and fields nearby in search of food and water.

It was often a dangerous life, taking what I needed to survive when, at times, it was not mine to take. I lost the use of a rear leg snatching a fish from the basket of a vendor in the marketplace when he sliced me with his knife. I managed to escape with my meal but the knife severed tendons and I am not able to support weight on that leg. Still, I was fortunate to keep my leg—and my life.

I was in a field of grain when I spotted a fat little mouse and my mouth watered. I moved quietly toward it, eagerly anticipating my next meal. It had been two days since my stomach last had food. The mouse was nibbling on a stalk, unaware of my presence and I was ready to pounce when it happened. I felt the irresistible calling of the Creator.

Leaving the mouse, I hurried through the field toward the road. It was there that I first saw him.

***

From a distance I follow him, trying to keep pace on only three good legs. The sun is high in the sky and the heat oppressive. I cough on the dust and long for water, but I press on, knowing I must catch up to him.

I keep my sight trained on him as he walks down the dusty road. People join him; first one, then a small group, and soon there is a large following. Some call out to him, pleading for him to help them, while others keep their silence, waiting for him to address them, guide them, lift their spirits.

I see him stop to rest beneath a large tree and I know this is my opportunity to catch up. It takes me some time but finally I sink into the softness of the grass beneath the shade of the immense tree. The Holy Man reaches down, palm cupped, and offers me water. I eagerly lap it up and continue licking his fingers until, chuckling, he scratches me behind the ear.

The crowd moves close around him, in part to seek shelter beneath the shade and in part to better hear. Sweat trickles off his chin and drips onto his sandal, making a small clean spot on the dust-covered footwear. He sets his walking stick on the ground beside him and smiles at the multitude, his lips stretching his brown skin, wrinkles forming at the corners of his mouth and eyes.

The gatherers quiet and he appears ready to speak when the shrill cry of an old woman pierces the air. She pleads to him for help. She is poor and sick, she says, "I beg your help." The crowd rebukes her, shouting her down, and a man pushes her away.

The Holy Man stands and raises his arms and the crowd quiets. "Let her be," he says calmly. The crowd seems startled by his decree and some grumble—but they comply, letting the woman stay on the edge of the group, though not allowing her entrance into it.

Lying on my side, I watch his mouth as he speaks, the facial hair curving as his lips form the words. He speaks quietly, almost shyly, as if conversing with an intimate acquaintance as he addresses the crowd. It's not the fiery oratory of others who tried to lead them and it's clear that this man is different. His message is not one of hate but rather one of love: peace over war, forgiveness over retaliation. When he finishes, all but a dozen disperse, returning to their daily lives while the man continues his journey.

"He's not the one," a man mumbles to his friend as they depart. "Someone else will need to lead us if we are to be free of the occupiers."

The occupiers. They came to us many years ago from their land, far away. We are but one small part of their empire, but a part they refuse to relinquish. The people have grown weary of them—many long to cast them out. But how? The people here are not a military power. No, sadly, they have become dependent on the occupiers. So they look for a leader, a savior to lead them to freedom.

Some believe it is this man, this gentle man, who will lead the rebellion. "He is very wise," they say. "He is a good man, a holy man. Surely God is with him," others reason. "His bravery cannot be questioned," some proclaim. "He does not cower from authority, though perhaps he should," another says quietly. "If he continues to excite the people, they will certainly kill him," still another assures them.

Kill him. Why? Because he teaches love, tolerance, and forgiveness? Isn't that what our Creator wants from us? The thought of harm coming to him makes me fear for him and I decide that I must stay close and watch over him.

We walk on until the sun is low in the sky. A follower offers to share a meal and he accepts. "Don't do it," those close to him advise. "You should not be seen with his kind," they admonish. "Only a crazy man would share a meal with the likes of him."

The one I follow shakes his head. He smiles, though I can see that it is a sad smile. "Do you really believe that one of God's children is lower than another? Lower because they were born into a poor family? Have you not listened to my messages?" and with that, joins his host.

His advisors are beside themselves with anger and I can't help but wonder how loyal they are to him. I decide that when he returns I will stay closer to the Holy Man and do what I can to protect him.

That evening, after prayers, I meander between his thin legs and he reaches down to stroke my head. Gently he pulls my tail as I change direction. He smiles at me. I purr loudly and he sighs. "Ah, to be so happy," he says in his quiet voice. I sense that in spite of the crowds that follow him and the few he confides in, that he is actually burdened and perhaps a bit lonely. That night, in spite of the heat, I curl up behind his knees and sleep against him.

And so goes each day: more walking and larger, more enthusiastic crowds come to hear the lessons he teaches—and more concern from those whose power he threatens. The more fame he gains, the more insecure and dangerous others become. He is not oblivious to the danger, but, rather, resigned to it. He proclaims that if he falls victim to violence, he will not be angry. "God must be in my heart and on my lips."

Often he leads his followers to the source of life itself—water—and, on the banks of the sacred river, delivers his sermons. I watch as he heals the sick and wonder at his empathy for those less fortunate, amazed at what he does to ease their burden. He teaches his followers the importance of self-sacrifice, hard work and faith; his life is an example of what he teaches.

As the days turn into weeks and the weeks into months, I marvel at what this man—this humble servant of the Creator—does to help others. Some say his accomplishments are heroic; others go as far as to call them miracles. And the crowds become larger, his fame more widespread, the jealousy and resentment more pronounced.

The occupiers brandish their military might in an effort to intimidate him and his followers. There is a great show of arms, as well as grandeur in their red and gold uniforms, reminding all that their empire is the greatest the world has ever known. The message they convey is clear: you are inferior; give up. But there is no quit in this man. Instead, he calls on the invaders to quit.

"Invaders quit? That would be the day." I hear them say. Some openly mock him and turn away in disgust. Others remain and listen to his message, wondering if somehow the seemingly impossible could be possible. Could, in the near future, they find themselves in a better world?

***

I walk to the doorway and peer into the eastern sky. I see the faintest of glows as the sun journeys toward us to start a new day. Soon I will hear the cock crow and the Master will rise to begin his day, first with a prayer, then with meditation and finally a meal. Normally, this would be a time to rejoice. The start of a new day. Even in these troubled times, my master brings hope to the people. But this day—this day, I sense, will be his last.

A cool pre-dawn breeze moves over me, ruffling my fur and bringing me relief, albeit temporary, from the heat. My ears twitch. What was that sound? Softly, as if carried by the breeze, I hear a voice. Sweet, melodic, it comforts me. In an ancient language it tells me to fear not, for this is all part of the Creator's plan.

I purr as this voice, this spirit, moves through me and my skin tingles The sky is changing from black to gray and finally, with the golden glow of the rising sun, to blue. I hear a cock crow in the distance, then another and another. In the upper room, I hear my master stir and, in spite of my knowledge that this is his last day with me, with this world, I am comforted.

***

I walk beside him, my head spinning, and my heart hopeful. The sun is almost setting as my master takes an evening walk, talking with those who surround him, offering hope. I don't understand. Did the Creator change the plan? Will my master stay longer on this earth to do the Creator's will? Did I misunderstand the message? Did I imagine it?

As I look at the faces of those around him, I see no enemies. Certain that there is no harm, I move toward the well. A young woman pours a small amount from the ladle onto the ledge of the well and I lap it up immediately. The coolness of the sweet water soothes my parched throat and, with that need cared for, I realize my hunger.

I glance around the crowded compound, certain that any rodents would be hiding in the tightest of places. My eyes are searching the walls of the houses, looking for small crevices, when I'm startled by the sudden report of three sharp cracks.

Screams break out and people are running everywhere. I look for my master but cannot see him in the pandemonium. Several men wrestle another to the ground, pulling something from his hand as they do. "My God," I hear someone scream. "He's dead. Gandhi is dead."

Life Seven ~ Attack on the Four Olds

The sun will not be up for another hour but Grandmother Ling wakes us before breakfast. "Get up," she tells us. "No more time for sleep, now time for prayers."

I yawn and stretch, and Jingfei does likewise, before moving toward the flickering light of candles in the next room. "Good morning, Grandma Ling," Jingfei says, taking her place near the candles. "Good morning Mama and Papa." Her smile lights the room far more than the candles. She is special, this one, I can tell.

Su Li lifts the portrait of Mao from the wall, flips it over and replaces it, revealing a painting of Buddha. The candlelight on either side illuminates the painting, a likeness that appears to me to be happy and wise. I much prefer this likeness to the other—to Mao, who always appears to be watching with suspicion and consternation.

While the others start their whispered prayers, I begin my search for breakfast. The apartment is small, only four small rooms, but the building is large and our apartment is only one floor above a restaurant, which guarantees a constant supply of mice and insects. Because I provide the valuable service of keeping the home pest-free, I am allowed to stay here, when I choose to do so.

Mostly the adults ignore me, but occasionally after witnessing my hunting skills they will bestow a smile upon me, and once Su Li stooped to pat my head and scratch behind my ears. But my Jingfei adores me, squealing with delight whenever I rub against her legs. She gently grabs my tail, allowing it to pass through her hand, and she coos, "Oh, Mama it is soft, like silk."

My hunt is successful and when I return morning prayers are completed and Hui, the man of the house, returns the portrait to its original position and blows out the candles before putting them away. No one must know of their morning ritual, for they live in the Forbidden City and here there is much forbidden, including private worship. Under the watchful eye of the Communists, religion is strictly controlled. Only two years earlier China invaded Tibet and drove their spiritual leader into exile. No one must challenge the Communists. Those who feel empowered through spirituality are likely to dissent, and those who are even suspected of dissention are imprisoned—or worse.

Grandma Ling remains sitting on the floor, staring into the flame of a candle she has lit. This candle and this time each morning are reserved for her husband, Heng, who died in the spring. It is a time for her to commune with him, in the ancient Chinese tradition.

I've heard Su Li tell Jingfei that they must have two faces, the public face that obeys the rules of the government, and the private face where tradition and spirituality are honored.

Su Li quickly goes about preparing breakfast while the others dress. As she is cooking the congee—a rice porridge—Hui appears before her in his neatly pressed white shirt, black trousers, his round spectacles covering sad brown eyes. He stares at the floor, his mouth pinched into a frown.

"You are troubled?" Su Li asks.

It is a few seconds before he responds, as if his mind was elsewhere and the question had to travel far to reach it. He blinks and turns his head to see who else may be nearby. "Yes," he says quietly. "I am troubled by the unrest at the University."

Su Li nods her head once but remains silent, waiting for her husband to continue if he so chooses. She stirs the congee before moving to the cabinet where she removes the bowls. She places them on a small tray in preparation for carrying them to the dining area.

"Remember how I told you about the student uprising in the summer? Well, at the time I thought it was a minor event, a debate gone awry. But now," he leans in close to his wife, his voice so low it can barely be heard, "Mao has recognized the political potential of the students. He is coming here to meet with them and I am greatly concerned that he will manipulate their passion and youthful energy into a destructive force. If he legitimizes them as a political force and convinces them to obey him," he shakes his head sadly, "he will use them to destroy his enemies."

Su Li's eyes grow wide. "His enemies?"

"Those in the government who rival him or have been critical of his failed policies," Hui explains. "These political battles have always turned into real wars with real people dying. The student movement is growing and Mao has called upon them to gather at Tiananmen Square on the 18th when he will speak to them. If Mao gives the students political authority, how will they ever be students again? Will they be interested in gaining knowledge when instead they could be gaining power?"

Su Li places a hand on his forearm and smiles at her husband. "How could they not be interested in gaining knowledge when they have you to learn from?"

I can tell from her expression that she is sincere. She truly adores Hui and believes him to be an irresistible force when it comes to imparting knowledge. Many evenings they have taken long slow walks through what was once Peking, but is now called Beijing, with Hui practicing the lectures he planned for his students, using her as his sounding board. Sometimes I tagged along to take in fresh air, fresh sights, fresh fish—but I digress. My point is, Hui *is* a great teacher and Su Li absolutely believes that students would be crazy not to continue their lessons with him. Ah, but power has a way of making people crazy, and young people suddenly gaining power in a culture that values experience could be ... dangerous.

***

Hui rushes into the apartment and quickly locks the door behind him. His hair is mussed, his clothes disheveled; perspiration gleams from his forehead. There are streaks of black on his cheeks and shirt, and his hands are blackened as well. He leans his back against the door, his breathing labored, and begins to shake.

Jingfei looks up from the book she is reading and frowns. "What is wrong, Papa?"

Hearing her, Su Li stops preparing dinner and comes into the room. "What is it?" she asks, her eyes wide. When Hui says nothing, she goes to him and pulls him into an embrace. "What's wrong?" she whispers in his ear.

I turn my head and my tail twitches as I watch them. This interaction is new and interesting.

Grandma Ling appears at my side, curious as to the meaning of the commotion. She is so quiet in her movements that she nearly startles me. Yes, I think, she would make a good cat.

As Su Li holds him, Hui's shaking stops, his breathing slows, and he looks around the room as if realizing for the first time where he was. When his gaze falls on Jingfei his right arm shoots out and he calls out

"Jingfei, come." She does so and he pulls her close to him, his left arm holding his wife. For several minutes no one speaks or moves until Hui quietly says, "We must talk. We can do so while we eat."

Grandma Ling disappears into the kitchen to finish preparing the meal and Su Li joins her, looking back over shoulder as she walks slowly to the kitchen. Jingfei returns to her books and Hui walks to the bathroom and closes the door.

When he opens it again he is clean and his hair is combed. He has removed his button-down shirt and stands in a T-shirt. I move closer to get a better look and as I brush against his leg, he reaches down and picks me up. I tense, as I am unsure of his intentions. Never before has he picked me up, or, for that matter, touched me at all. He turns my head to look at me, his face calm, and I relax as I realize he means me no harm. He looks into my eyes and I into his. I see it … compassion.

Shifting his grip on me, Hui cradles me in one arm and strokes my head with his free hand. Slowly he walks into the next room and stands near Jingfei. She looks up from her book and smiles. "You like Qingling?" she asks, revealing to her father what had been up to now our secret—the name she has given me.

He kneels down and places me in her lap. Giving me a quick scratch behind my ears he says "Yes, Jingfei, I like Qingling."

Jingfei giggles and gives me hug, burying her face in the fur of my neck. It tickles.

Our reverie is interrupted by food as Su Li and Grandma Ling bring in dishes of rice, fish, and shrimp for the humans. I notice the movement of a mouse against the far wall and soon we are *all* enjoying a nice meal.

The meal starts with a prayer and the serving of food as everyone waits for Hui to speak. When he does, his voice is soft like snowfall but his words crack like thunder. "Today the Red Guard, as the students call themselves, began their attack on the Four Olds. At Mao's urging, they seek to destroy traditional ways in China and replace them with Mao's version of a Communistic society. They are to attack old customs, old culture, old habits, and old ideas. And who decides what is to be attacked? They do."

His words come out as if being squeezed from his throat and he pauses to sip from his tea. As he does, I watch Grandma Ling and Su Li exchange wide-eyed glances.

"This morning before classes, all faculty was assembled and given new instructions. Instead of Confucius, we are to teach Mao," he said pulling a small red book from his shirt pocket, placing it on the floor in front of him. "Then they gathered our texts, placed them in a pile in the yard … and set fire to them. Some of us tried to pull books out of the flames but we were not successful. When the Master demanded they stop, he was taken away. No one has seen him since. Many doubt that we ever will." As he finished these words he bowed his head for a full minute, then continued.

"We were told that non-compliance would not be tolerated. I heard a leader giving instructions. Anything pre-dating 1949 is subject to being destroyed. Intellectuals are to be targeted. Western ways will be eradicated.

"But that makes no sense," Su Li interjected. "We were told that the Western ways are decadent because they honor the selfishness of modern materialism. I might understand that, but the intellectuals promote modern thinking only as solutions to problems within our system. And the Four Olds, they are our heritage, our history, our culture. They are who we are. Attacking intellectuals and destroying the Four Olds would be contradictory—attacking the old and the new. It makes no sense."

"Do not expect this to make sense," Hui warns. "This is not a logical step to progression; it is a way to destroy enemies." He looks at each face one by one. "We must be very careful as there is no way to know who they will target." His eyes rest on Jingfei. "Do you understand what I am telling you?"

She nods her head.

"Then promise me that you not speak out or do anything to draw attention to yourself. Promise me."

Jingfei looks at him, her brown eyes sad. "I promise."

***

"Button your coat," Hui tells Jingfei. "Don't let the bright sunshine fool you, it is very cold outside."

"Yes, Papa," Jingfei says as her small nimble fingers quickly button her coat. "After the gallery, can we go to the temple? The sculptures there are so beautiful."

"Perhaps," Hui answers, "if time permits."

I slip past them as they leave the apartment and descend the stairs, pausing at the bottom, just inside the doorway. "Do you have your book?" Hui inquires.

Jingfei pulls the little red book from her pocket and holds it up for Hui to see.

"Very good," Hui says with a sigh.

I wait beneath the stairs until Hui opens the door to the street, then scamper out. I start to head toward the market where the sounds and smells are alluring but something stops me. I look over my shoulder and see Hui and Jingfei walk in the opposite direction, toward the Chaobai River. Something compels me to follow, and so I do.

They cross a bridge over the river and continue straight ahead in a westerly direction. The sun at my back warms me against the chill of the morning air. When I reach the summit of the bridge, I see that the mountains that run west to north, are covered with snow halfway down. I also notice a plume of smoke straight ahead in the distance, just above the rooftops at the far end of the city. I hurry so as not to lose sight of Hui and Jingfei.

As always, the streets are crowded and at times I find it difficult to discern their presence through the mass of humanity. At this distance humans are like snowflakes, each unique but hard to distinguish with the naked eye. I train my eye to look lower, to look for Jingfei. She is wearing a yellow coat, and, in her hair, a silk ribbon from her Grandmother Ling. There! I move as quickly as is possible through the crowd, careful to keep her in my vision. We cross a side street and finally I am caught up with them.

"Oh, no," I hear Hui say in a choked voice. I can smell the smoke now, acrid and rancid, and hear the crackling of burning wood. We stop behind a small group of people but I cannot see past them. A man and woman turn and leave, tears streaming down the face of the woman. We move forward to the place in front that they had vacated.

"What … Papa, are they … no," Jingfei cries. She buries her face against Hui's side and he puts a protective arm around her. I blink my eyes to focus on the scene in front of us.

Young men, some with torches, stand in a circle around a large bonfire. As I try to see what is fueling the flames another man exits the building carrying a large painting, and, on his heels, another carrying a wood sculpture. They step up to the circle and heave the items into the fire. The group cheers. "Destroy the old," a voice cries out. "Cultural Revolution for a new China," calls out another. "Mao is great," another voice proclaims. Soon a chant begins, "Red Guard, Red Guard, Red Guard, Red Guard."

Hui picks up Jingfei and shoulders back out through the crowd. He says nothing and his walk is stiff, as if sleepwalking. Jingfei has her face against Hui's neck, but I still hear her sobs and feel the wetness of her tears as they fall upon me. The walk home is long, slow and laborious. The heaviness of our hearts adds so much weight it feels as if we are walking up a mountain carrying a load of bricks.

When we finally make it home, we are exhausted. Jingfei goes straight to bed, refusing Su Li's plea to eat first. I, too, have lost my appetite and slip into her room to curl up next to her on the mattress. In the next room I hear Hui's low voice recounting to Su Li and Grandma Ling the tragedy we have witnessed. I fall into a troubled sleep.

***

"She's exhausted," Hui whispers as he lays Jingfei on her bed, adjusting the pillow under her neck. Su Li carefully places the small carved figurine on top of the bookshelf before moving to her husband's side. They stand, silently watching their daughter sleep, and I can see the love on their faces. For a long time they watch Jingfei, and I watch them.

"It was a big day for her," Su Li says. "Thank you for making her day so special."

Hui shrugs his shoulders. "It was special for me, too, seeing her so happy," he says, a grin playing at the corner of his mouth.

Su Li rests her head on his shoulder and he slips an arm around her. "I'm sure she will always remember the trip to Nanking," Su Li says. "The magic of her first train ride and all the sights along the way."

"I'm glad we could do it," Hui says. "I'm glad we were able to visit a heritage site before they are all destroyed."

I see Su Li tense at these words and a frown appears on her face.

"Do you really think that will happen?"

Hui replies, "According to the last census, there were six thousand eight hundred and forty-three heritage sites. According to the Cultural Minister, over four thousand nine hundred have been destroyed."

Su Li turns to leave the room and Hui follows. When they are alone in their own room Su Li asks, "Why do they destroy our country's treasures? I don't understand how that will make us great."

"It won't," Hui answers as he removes his eyeglasses and rubs his eyes. "Destroying our heritage in some vain hope of establishing a new culture is," he steps toward his wife and whispers in her ear so that even someone—other than a cat, of course—in the room with them could not hear, "madness."

Su Li's eyes grow very wide but she says nothing. She puts her arms around her husband's neck as he continues to whisper.

"Our leaders want to be a world power, equal to the likes of the Soviets and America. They boast of the nuclear detonation we recently achieved and of advances in other technology, yet they allow—no, they *encourage*—youth to destroy that which has truly made us great: our art, our scholarship, our heritage."

Su Li moves her lips close to his ear until they are nearly touching. "Please, I beg you, don't ever let anyone else hear you say that. Bury those feelings inside you. Your truth will only bring us sorrow."

***

Jingfei stands outside the school and stares into the distance past the Great Wall at the mountains. The snow has receded, with only the faintest of lines still visible at the top. She doesn't seem to notice the young man on the corner watching her. But I do, and I'm watching him. He has a small notebook, the kind used at university, and occasionally makes frantic notations. Dressed in black trousers and button-down shirt with matching shoes, he is conspicuous, though apparently not to Jingfei.

She turns around and begins walking slowly toward home. The man, a boy really, probably not yet out of his teen years, scribbles in his notebook, allowing her a generous head start before following. I choose a path on the opposite side of the street halfway between them.

It is not far to home and Jingfei takes her time, stopping to look at the machines building a new tower, waving at a friend looking down from her apartment, and staring in wonder at an automobile as it passes. Each of her actions is recorded by her observer and I wonder why. What makes Jingfei so interesting to this man?

When she enters the building that houses her apartment, the man trots after her, stopping outside the door and, seeing the number, writes furiously in his notebook. Once he has finished his note, he snaps the book closed and, smiling, walks down the street, disappearing around a corner.

That evening I stand watch, but the man does not return. Days turn into weeks and nothing extraordinary happens. On occasion Hui whispers to Su Li about a colleague who has been taken away, or about the rumors of mass executions in other cities, but, for this family, life is unchanged.

One evening Hui returns home smiling and animated. He picks Jingfei up and twirls her around and she squeals with delight. Su Li and Grandma Ling come into the room to see for themselves what the causes the commotion. Seeing them, Hui calls out, "Come, let us celebrate." He sets Jingfei down and positions the ladies in a circle with him, hand in hand, and begins to move in a circle, singing a song and dancing a celebratory dance that was passed down generation to generation in his family.

Su Li smiles broadly as they dance, for it has been a very long time since they have found cause to celebrate. She exaggerates her movements for the benefit of Jingfei who was so young the last time they danced that she doesn't remember the steps. It is a simple dance, though, and Jingfei quickly picks up the repetitious movements, smiling more broadly as she masters it.

When Hui finishes the song, they embrace each other before Grandma Ling returns to preparing dinner and Jingfei to her studies. Alone with Hui, Su Li asks, "What are we celebrating, dear husband?"

Hui grins. "Better days." He takes Su Li by the hand and leads her to their room where he pulls her close to him and says quietly, though not quite in a whisper, "Today the Party leaders have condemned the 'Cultural Revolution' and have ordered the Red Guard to stop the destruction of the heritage sites. There is also talk of the army being used to restore order. Soon all will be back to normal. There is even talk that more freedom will be granted. Perhaps the bell is finally swaying back our way."

A full season goes by and things are definitely getting better. Each evening, Hui brings news of the fighting between Maoist and anti-Maoist, which he assures us will result in an end to the attack on the Four Olds and the repression. "The Red Guard, though still present in the schools and Universities, appears to be content to observe without taking action," he tells us, smiling. To Jingfei he says "Maybe this year for your birthday we can take you to visit a temple. I know of one in the mountains that is truly magnificent. They say the spirits are strong there and you can feel them so powerfully it is magical."

That night I wander the building in the reassuring calm of the darkness. I think about Jingfei and her family and decide that they do not need me. Of course, I will still check in on Jingfei, just to ensure she is doing well. But tonight I feel free to live my own life. Perhaps it is time for me to start my own family.

***

As I descend the stairs in the morning the hair on my back stands up. Something is wrong. The door to the apartment is open—something they would never do. I scurry in and stop abruptly. The apartment is in disarray with things scattered about and the painting—the two-sided one—is missing.

I run from room to room, calling out in the vain hope that they are still here. Perhaps they are hiding. "Come out," I meow. "You are safe now." But they are not safe, as they are not here. My heart sinks.

I go to Jingfei's room and sit on her mattress and breathe in her scent. They have taken her figurine and the pictures she had drawn which she had hung on the wall; her clothes are strewn about. I hang my head and cover my eyes with my paws because I know in my heart that I have failed her. I have failed her and her family and now I will never see them again.

Life Eight ~ The Tainted Birthday

Kelli Parker absently strokes my back as I sit on her lap. She gazes out the window. It's a beautiful late summer day and the cool breeze coming across the Long Island Sound makes what would otherwise be a hot day very comfortable. People pass by on the street below, but she doesn't take notice, her thoughts somewhere else on this lovely day.

I rub my face against her hand and purr to encourage her to continue petting me. It's so good to have her home, though soon she will return for her senior year at Brown to finish her studies before she can return home for good. I have missed her so much. I lick her hand and she smiles down at me and scratches me behind my ears.

Her mother is very proud of Kelli and the young woman she has become. Once a frightened and angry pre-teen, she has matured into a thoughtful and reserved young woman, though a little bit shy. According to her mother, she is studious and near the top of her class academically. She's the type of girl more interested in attending a play than a party, more comfortable thinking about her schoolwork than about dating.

It isn't as if she doesn't have opportunities, mind you. She isn't drop-dead gorgeous, though most people describe her as pretty. Her brown hair is parted in the middle and frames her oval face. It falls over her shoulders and down her back where it ends at her shoulder blades. Black-framed rectangular glasses give her a serious look and partially obscure the large brown eyes that poets would describe as "doe like." She has a hint of freckles that form a band at the top of her cheeks and across the bridge of her nose, which has a gentle upturn at its tip.

She kisses the top of my head, then gently moves me from her lap to the bed, stands up, and stretches. She walks to her closet and rummages through it until she emerges with a shoebox. She blows dust from the lid, walks to the bed and sits down, the shoebox in her lap. Slowly removing the lid, she reaches in and picks up an envelope and stares at it.

She takes the contents out of the envelope and re-reads the cover letter, now yellow and brittle with age. She carefully removes the essay she had submitted, smoothing the folds with her hand, when her solitude is interrupted by a text message on her phone.

Reading the message, she smiles. I meow to get her attention and she looks at me and says, "It's Rachel. You remember her, don't you, boy?"

Indeed I do. Rachel was one of Kelli's best friends throughout junior high and high school. Before they graduated and went to separate schools, Kelli, Rachel, and another girl, Courtney, were inseparable friends. Now, they get in touch when all are home, which is only a few times a year.

Kelli deftly types a message and hits the send key and almost instantly receives a reply. This exchange continues another three or four times before Kelli stops and just stares at the message.

Curious, I move closer so that I can see the message. *"Is ur mom ok w'it?*

Kelli draws a deep breath and speaks to me. "I haven't told her. I haven't decided when I'm going to."

I shake my head, not understanding, and she rubs my cheeks with her thumbs before typing a response to Rachel.

There is another flurry of messages exchanged before Kelli sets down the phone and pulls me into her lap. "I know I need to tell her soon, but I don't know how," she whispers before planting a kiss on my head.

***

"Hey, Leonardo," Rachel calls and reaches out to me. I nuzzle her hand as she exclaims, "I think it's so cool that you named your cat after DiCaprio."

"Da Vinci," Kelli corrects, "not DiCaprio"

The two giggle at the replay of the conversation they first had in seventh grade.

"I know," Courtney interrupts excitedly, her black hair swaying, "you should have a party. It'll be awesome. I'll handle everything, just leave it to me. Wait," she gasps as if receiving a divine epiphany, "we'll have it at the Yacht Club."

Kelli can't help smiling at her friend's enthusiasm even as she holds up a hand to stop her.

"What?" Courtney asks, looking bemused.

"Look, I think it's sweet of you and all, but I really don't want a party," Kelli tells her. She pulls me into her lap and gently strokes my ears. I love that and purr loudly so that she understands she has my permission to continue for as long as she likes.

Courtney looks at Rachel incredulously and Rachel takes up the cause. "It doesn't have to be a formal party. We can have it at my place, or, wait, I know, we can use the community center. We'll decorate it and invite only your family and closest friends. We'll have a nice dinner catered and a band. My brother's band is always looking for gigs and would probably do it for free."

"Hey, listen, you guys are wonderful—the best friends in the world, honestly. But I really don't want a party. I really don't know how this is going to go over with everyone," she says, looking away.

The other girls frown and for a moment the only sound is my purring. The porch swing creaks as Courtney gets up and comes to stand next to Kelli. She puts her hand on Kelli's shoulder and softly says, "Look, Kell, I know this is awkward. I mean, I can't imagine what you and your mom have gone through and all but, well, you know, this is a special day for you. It's a celebration of your life. You deserve to enjoy it."

Kelli lays her cheek against Courtney's hand. "Thanks," she whispers, "but no."

Courtney sighs and returns to the swing. There is silence for a long time and eventually the warm sun and the awesome ear rub lull me into a peaceful sleep. I awaken when Kelli picks me up from her lap and carries me inside. The girls, now women about to graduate from university, are heading down the sidewalk and the sun is starting its westward descent.

The phone rings and Kelli answers on the third ring. "Hello," she says, followed by silence as she listens to the caller. She glances at the clock on the mantle and says, "Okay, Mom, see you then," and hangs up the phone.

She releases me and I stretch out my legs before following her into the kitchen. I watch from the counter as she removes containers from the freezer, preheats the oven, and sets the table. She leafs through her mother's *New Yorker* as she waits for the oven. A chime lets her know when it's ready and she quickly places the dishes inside and sets the timer.

She leaves the kitchen and starts up the stairs. I call out, but she ignores me. How will she ever hear the timer from up there?

After a moment I follow her up the stairs where I find her sitting at her desk, looking at the essay. She bites her lower lip and her brow is creased in concentration. She looks again at the calendar on the wall, then down at me. "I'm going to do it, Leonardo." She reaches out to pet me. "Tonight after dinner, I'm telling Mom."

I hop up on the bed and curl against the pillow. I'm flooded by the memory of her sixteenth birthday, when Kelli first wrote the essay. As she takes her cell phone and walks to the bathroom I enter into an almost trancelike state.

It's 2006 again. Kelli looks at me and asks, "Will you help me prepare, Leonardo? I need to practice reading aloud." My look answers her question. "Good, then let's get started."

Kelli looks around the room and spots her music stand next to her violin case in the corner against the dresser. She brings it in front of the desk and places the essay on it. She wipes her hands off on her jean shorts, clasps them together behind her back, and clears her throat. "The Tainted Birthday," she begins.

"It was a beautiful mid September day and I was filled with excitement as I sat in Sister Margaret's sixth grade homeroom. This was the day I looked forward to more than any other during the year, even more than Christmas. This was my birthday, my eleventh birthday.

"I fidgeted in my seat as roll call was taken, unable to push images of balloons, cake, ice cream, and presents from my mind. My dad had promised to take us to Medieval Times for dinner and I looked forward to watching the tournament and cheering for my favorite knight. 'What better place for a princess to be on her special day,' he had teased me at breakfast that morning. I had no idea that it would be the last time I would see him alive."

Kelli rocked on her heals nervously and she swallowed hard before continuing. "It was approximately nine fifteen in the morning when the intercom interrupted math class and we were told to assemble in the cafeteria. At the time, I was thrilled. I hated math class. As the students filed in, the teachers were gathered into a corner with our principal, Father Anthony. He was talking to them and I noticed some of the teachers cover their mouths with their hands while others crossed themselves. It scared me.

"When everyone was assembled, Father Anthony informed us that we would be evacuating the building and that he needed all of us to listen to our teachers and follow their instructions. He said that an accident had occurred at the World Trade Center and that we would be going to Saint Michael's, several blocks north of our school. 'Staff members will be calling your parents to let them know where to pick you up,' he informed us. And he assured us that everything would be fine."

At this, Kelli paused and I could see her hand shake as she turned the page. She inhaled deeply, slowly exhaled, and inhaled again before continuing. "Everything was not fine. On the street we could see smoke and flames from the towers and people were rushing past us, some crying, some shrieking, nearly all moving away from the towers. We soon learned that it was not an accident at the World Trade Centers, but rather a terrorist attack. This news pushed us to the brink of panic.

"I remember Sister Margaret reassuring us as she led us away from the school, her calm demeanor giving me strength. We passed other children being led from their schools and, in retrospect, it is amazing that the evacuation of approximately eight thousand school children went as well as it did.

"It wasn't until we reached Saint Michael's that I really had time to think. Outside things were too chaotic, too noisy for any kind of thought other than to get to safety. Inside the quiet of the church, I thought about my father for the first time since the attack. My father worked in the south tower at the WTC.

"My mother arrived to pick me up around ten thirty. I could tell she'd been crying. When she saw me, she pulled me into her arms and held me so tightly it was difficult to breathe. She stroked my hair and kissed my face repeatedly before taking my hand and leading me outside. I asked her if Daddy was safe, but she didn't answer. Our apartment was only a few blocks from the WTC, so there was no way we could return there. Mom told me we were going to my Aunt Kate's house on Long Island. I remember her telling me we'd be safe there.

"We walked quickly, nearly running, as we headed to Penn Station. We passed an electronics store with televisions on display in front. She got between the store and me, took my hand and pulled me quickly past, telling me to hurry so we wouldn't miss our train. I later learned it was so I wouldn't see that the south tower had collapsed.

"I asked her if Daddy had called on his cell phone and her lip trembled when she told me he had not. She insisted that we had nothing to worry about; he probably couldn't get through because the communications were jammed. I remember asking her why, what was happening? Her answer was a curt 'Hatred. That's what's happening.'

"We arrived at the Stony Brook Station a little after noon, having to transfer twice during our trip. I'd heard people talking, saying the towers had both collapsed and that the Pentagon, too, had been attacked. While the prevailing emotion was fear, it was during this trip that I saw the first signs of anger and calls for revenge.

"At the station, my Aunt Kate met us and drove us to her home where I was finally allowed to watch the news of the attack. I was crying as I realized that the building where my dad worked was now completely demolished and that hundreds, perhaps thousands, were dead."

Kelli paused and wiped a tear from her eye as she tried to regain her composure. I couldn't move. I could barely breathe. Finally, she continued.

"Mom continued to try to reach Dad's cell phone but the lines were all busy. We started hearing reports that many from the towers had been safely evacuated before their collapse and Aunt Kate squeezed my mom's hand and gave her a hopeful smile. I was still watching the news, but when they showed the video of people jumping from the towers, my mom shut off the television. I went to bed in my aunt's spare room and cried myself to sleep.

"I woke up around seven o'clock that night, my stomach rumbling since I hadn't eaten anything since breakfast. My mom's cell phone rang and I immediately ran to her asking, 'Is it Daddy?' After saying hello and confirming her identity, she was silent. A few seconds later she slumped to the floor, letting the phone slip from her fingers as she covered her mouth in horror. It was at that exact moment that I knew my father was dead."

Kelli is openly weeping now, the tears streaming down her cheeks. She walks to the bed and sits beside me, her hands trembling as she reaches for me. I allow her to pick me up and hold me in her arms against her chest as she buries her face into my fur. I can feel her tears and know that her heart is breaking as she relives that moment. I would cry with her, if I could.

A few moments later, she whispers, "I don't know if I can do this, Leonardo. I don't know if I'm strong enough." I look into her eyes, trying to tell her that she is. She is stronger than she knows.

The timer on the oven chimes, bringing me back to the present. Kelli quickly ends her phone call and returns downstairs to the kitchen. The smell of the roast and potatoes wafts through the air when she opens the oven door. I immediately salivate. Kelli finishes setting the food out when I hear footsteps on the porch. "Hi, Kelli," calls her mom as the front door swings open.

"Hi, Mom," Kelli answers. "How was your day?"

"Fine, Sweetie," her mother replies as she comes into the kitchen. Holding her briefcase in one hand, she gives Kelli a hug, then looks at the table. "Honey, this looks delicious and I'm starved. Let me clean up and we'll eat."

Mrs. Parker takes the briefcase and heads up the stairs. Kelli looks in the mirror and sees on her cheeks the tracks left by her tears. She goes to the sink, turns on the faucet, and splashes water on her face before drying it with a dishtowel. She checks the mirror again and, satisfied that it's the best she can do, sits down at the table.

A few minutes later her mother returns. They hold hands across the table, bow their heads, and say grace before dishing up the food. "What did you do today, Kell, anything exciting?"

Kelli shrugs as she slices some roast and puts it on her plate. "Not really. Courtney and Rachel came over and we sat on the porch and talked for a while. This morning I practiced the violin and I surfed the Net a bit—nothing too exciting. How about you?"

"Same old thing," Mrs. Parker replies. "Took orders, negotiated with vendors, and bought supplies." She smiles at Kelli. "Just trying to keep everyone at the hospital happy."

Kelli smiles back. She loves her mother, who has been a rock for her through all the bad times, the move from Manhattan, changing schools, grief counseling, and transition from child to young woman. She loves her mother and wishes she could find peace and happiness.

I remember sitting on Kelli's lap on the top of the stairs, outside her mother's bedroom. Kelli held me tight and rocked back and forth as her mother cried softly in her room. That was nine years ago on the anniversary of Mr. Parker's death—and eight years ago, and every year since. It will undoubtedly be this year as well.

I meander between their legs while they eat, rubbing myself against them and hoping for scraps. The only thing I get is a quick scratch behind the ears from Mrs. Parker before she starts to clear the table.

An hour after dinner, Kelli tells her mom that they need to talk, that she has something important to tell her. Mrs. Parker nods absently and brushes her cheek with the back of her hand. Kelli looks closely at her mom before walking up to her and giving her an embrace. "It can wait," she whispers.

***

That night I dream of Kelli's birthday five years before, and the dream is so real it feels more like déjà vu than a dream.

Kelli puts on a summer dress and fixes her hair in the mirror. The ceremony is at one o'clock in the afternoon, in the outdoor amphitheater at the community college just a few blocks away. Rachel and Courtney promised to be there for support and, of course, I'll be there, too, invited or not.

Kelli smoothes her dress with her hands and checks her reflection in the mirror. Satisfied, she walks to the desk and picks up her essay, checking each page to ensure nothing is missing. She looks at me and says, "Wish you could be there, Leonardo," and pats my head, keeping me at arm's length so that I don't get hair all over her. Oh, I'll be there, all right.

I make my way to the kitchen and climb onto the windowsill. I push the screen with my head and it surrenders a space large enough for me to slide through. I jump to the ground and dart through the hedges that separate the properties. This is almost too easy. I crouch low next to the hedge and listen as Kelli shuts and locks the front door. I see her pass and wait until she is three houses away before following. I stay out of sight, choosing bushes and trees to scamper next to so that she won't see me and be tempted to take me back. She doesn't notice. She is reading the essay again as she walks.

Kelli goes to the stage and speaks to a woman in a navy blue linen jacket. The woman listens, then checks some papers on her clipboard before directing Kelli to a seat in the front row of the audience. There are four other young adults there, all high school students, and they smile nervously when the lady addresses them.

A crowd is slowly entering the amphitheater, spreading out through the empty seats, which become fewer and fewer with each passing moment. The lady in the blue linen jacket tests the microphone at the podium and gives a thumbs up sign to someone in the back. A team of students has set up a camera in the back row and the boy next to Kelli points it out. The five young people look, and I can't tell if their expressions show excitement or horror.

Someone notices me and tries to pet me but I scurry away. I find a nice shade tree at the edge of the amphitheater and I scamper up to a wide branch that is out of reach for anyone on the ground and affords me an unobstructed view of the stage. I decide to clean myself as I wait for the ceremony to begin.

I hear excited chatter and notice that Courtney and Rachel have arrived. They chat a moment with Kelli until the lady in the blue linen jacket makes her way to the podium and the girls take their seats a few rows behind the readers.

The atmosphere is somber, almost like a church service. The speaker introduces herself as Mary Jackson, President of the College, and welcomes everyone. "Five years ago today all of our lives were changed by a series of tragic events. I am, of course, referring to the terrorist attacks of September 11, 2001. Today we gather together to commemorate the event, to honor the heroes of that day, and to get a better understanding of how our lives have been irrevocably altered."

She pauses and takes a sip of water from a glass that sits on a shelf inside the podium. She returns the glass before speaking. "I'd like to begin by inviting to the stage Father John Ashton, Reverend William Cox, Rabbi Daniel Cohen, and Imam Abdul-Salam, for some *brief*," she emphasizes the word and raises her eyebrows, causing the audience to chuckle, "remarks."

The distinguished speakers all took their turns speaking about the events of 9-11 and calling for peace and unity. This was followed by a moment of silence in memory of those who lost their lives that fateful day. Many in the crowd wiped tears from their eyes as Ms. Jackson returned to the podium.

"We are honored today to have five very bright, articulate students with us to share their stories. They were selected from over five hundred entrants, and their stories are, in my opinion, amazing. These are the personal stories of each reader, and reflect the profound effect the events of 9-11 has had on their lives. Our first reader will be Orlando Martinez."

From my vantage point I could see that the first reader sat to the left of Kelli, and, if the order continued, she would read second. My deduction was further supported by the way she fidgeted in her seat, struggling to be attentive to her predecessor, who spoke for a few minutes, relating his story of being a military brat whose father was sent to Afghanistan to fight on the front lines of the "war on terrorism." His father had come home and had later been redeployed, first to Iraq, and later returned to Afghanistan before retiring recently. The young man stated that it was his intention to follow in his father's steps and join the Army after graduation. The audience applauded heartily when he concluded.

As Kelli made her way to the podium, I could see that her legs were shaking. She drew in a slow, deep breath before starting. As she read her essay, the audience was silent, except for the occasional sniffle.

"For me, as for all of us, life must go on. For some, it's more difficult than others. My mother has protected me and nurtured me, helping me adjust to a new school and life in a new town where reminders of that day, that tragedy, are less stark. Through this, she grieves in silence. Yes, she's participated in grief counseling and, yes, she still does. But we never talk about my father or what his loss has meant to her. Each year on the anniversary of that day, we silently grieve his loss instead of celebrating my life."

She concluded with, "For me, 9-11 will always be a day of sadness and my birthday will always be tainted."

She walked off the stage to silence.

I watched her as she returned to her seat and I could see her physically relax, the burden of the reading removed. She sat upright, listening with apparent interest to the students that followed her. The last speaker, a young woman named Dalal Saleh, stood at the podium looking very nervous. She looked at the audience, swallowed hard, and began.

"I was eleven years old, attending public school in Bay Ridge, not far from Fort Hamilton. My father, Baruk, a taxicab driver, came to this country in 1977 from Afghanistan and met my mother a year later. A year after that they married, and the following year I was born. In Afghanistan, before the Taliban, my father owned a shop and his family had money. In America, my father was poor, but he was happy. 'We have two things more important than money, Dalal,' he would tell me. 'We have freedom and opportunity.'"

She glanced up from her paper to look at the audience, her large brown eyes apprehensive. Her focus returned to her paper and she continued. "On that day, my father drove me to school in his taxi. He was so proud that I was getting an education. 'You can be whatever you want in this country, Dalal. Well, maybe not President, but almost anything else,' he would say with a laugh.

"On that fateful day, we learned the news from our principal, Ms. Carter. We would not evacuate as had many of the schools in Manhattan, but, instead, we were being sent home. 'Pray,' she urged us, 'pray for our country.'

"I walked home that morning, since my father was occupied with taking military members to Fort Hamilton, refusing their payments, proud to help his country in the only way he knew how. My mother was waiting for me at home and sat me down in the living room to talk to me. She told me that terrorists had attacked our country and that it was suspected they were Islamic militants. She explained to me that some people, a small minority, had taken a violent interpretation of the Holy Quran, something I just couldn't fathom. These people were intent on destroying everyone who did not share their beliefs. She cried as she told me these things.

"Then my mother held me in her arms and made me promise to be careful. She shared her fear that some people, people who did not know us for who we were, people who were afraid and angry, might do us harm. She told me to stay close to home and in the company of friends. She told me not to defend myself if someone confronted me, but rather to seek a safe place. She informed me that we would not be attending worship services because she was afraid it would be a target of those seeking revenge. My mother's words filled me with dread.

"That night, my father came home looking very grim. While he had spent the better part of the day giving free taxi rides to military members, his last trip to Fort Hamilton was turned away. The guards at the gate had eyed him suspiciously and detained him while they checked his ID. My father was humiliated, but, worse than that, he was afraid.

"In the coming weeks, each day became more difficult. I had trouble sleeping. My father found it hard to find fares; people would refuse entry into his taxi. Some looked at him with fear, others with contempt. He told my mother he wasn't sure which hurt worse. At the end of the week, my father was fired from his job.

"For me, school wasn't much better. Many of my 'friends' stopped talking to me and I learned that a group of mothers had petitioned the school to have the 'Middle Eastern' children removed. Ms. Carter adamantly refused, threatening to resign if the school board took such an action. I will always be grateful for her courage.

"At home, things were becoming increasingly tense. My father looked for work every day but could not find any. Sometimes he would be jeered as cars passed him on the street and once someone threw a bottle at him, narrowly missing him. He changed a little each day. No more laughter or teasing. Instead he was grim, his face creasing with frown lines, adding years to his appearance.

"My mother asked him if we should consider returning to Afghanistan and I thought he would explode. 'How can we return? Why would we want to? Do you want to get killed by the bombs being dropped or to suffer at the hands of the Taliban? No. This is our home, this is where we stay.'

"At the end of the month, my father made his last payment of our rent. He had depleted his entire savings providing for his family. Unable to find work, he turned to those from the Middle East. They were all suffering as he had, with only a few of the more educated people, those with established jobs in high demand industries, being unaffected.

"In November we lived off the graciousness of others. My father kept notes on who had given us food or money so that one day, when things got better, he could repay them. He talked to everyone he knew asking, 'Do you know where I can find work? I'll do anything, anything.' They just shook their heads sadly. Since 9-11, and with the passage of the Patriot Act, finding a job was nearly impossible.

"The last week of November, my father came home very excited. A man had seen him on the street looking for work and had stopped to talk to him. The man bought my father a cup of coffee and learned that my father had driven a taxi. 'So, you are a driver. Perfect. I need someone to make deliveries for me,' my father recounted in laughter. 'Praise Allah, he has not forsaken us.' It was the first time in nearly three months that I had heard the sound of his laughter, seen him smile.

"The laughter, the money, the hope, all of it soon vanished. A week after my father started, his delivery van was stopped by the police. A thorough search turned up drugs, hidden within some of the items. Of course, my father had no idea that he was being used as part of a drug smuggling operation, but apparently the police did. They had been watching the operation for quite a while and now were ready to bring it down. They wanted my father to give them information on the others, but he honestly didn't know anything. In the end, they told him he was suspected of using the money to help fund terrorism and that his case would be turned over to the FBI.

"My father's note to my mother was brief. 'They have taken my honor. I have nothing else to give.' He hung himself in a jail cell with the bed sheets."

At this Dalal, dabbed at her eyes with a handkerchief and struggled to regain her composure. After a collective gasp, the audience grew silent.

"The victims of 9-11 are many," she continued, "but we do our best to pick up the pieces and go on. Every day I try to make a new friend, show them who I really am: a kind person, not someone to be feared. If asked, I share some knowledge about my religious beliefs. They are probably not that different from yours. I try to do what my father taught me: seek first to understand, then to be understood. Through understanding, we become one. Thank you."

As Dalal was leaving the stage, there was a delay as her words sunk in. Then the audience broke into thunderous applause and people began to stand, until all were standing. Ms. Jackson stopped Dalal at the edge of the stage and held her hand. She motioned for the other readers to join them and when they did, all joined hands. She raised their hands in triumph, before stepping to the microphone and saying simply, "Thank you for coming."

***

In the morning, I awaken to find Kelli sitting at her desk re-reading her essay from five years ago. Her eyes are moist when she finishes and sets the pages aside. I jump up on the desk and she chuckles. "Well, good morning, Leonardo," she says as she tousles my head. I push the essay with my paws and she says, "Oh, do you remember this?"

I meow my answer and she giggles. She picks me up and embraces me. I snuggle my head beneath her chin and breathe in her scent. I want this moment to last forever and I get the feeling she does, too. "Tonight my life will change, Leonardo," she says quietly, though I have no idea what means.

She sets me down and goes downstairs with me following close behind. In the kitchen she says, "Good morning, Mom," and pours herself a cup of coffee.

"Happy Birthday, Sweetheart," her mother answers, putting the morning paper aside. "So what big plans do you have today?"

"Courtney and Rachel are springing for a spa treatment," Kelli says, smiling.

"That sounds absolutely wonderful," he mother says rising from the table.

Kelli looks into her mother's blue eyes and hesitates as if trying to decide something. "Do you remember when I said I had something to tell you?"

"No, Sweetie, I'm sorry. What is it?"

Kelli grips the back of a chair leans on it for support. "I know that usually it's just the two of us," she begins, "but tonight I want someone to join us for dinner."

Mrs. Parker nods as she walks to the coat closet to retrieve her briefcase. "Sure, Sweetie, whatever you want," she says, though I see one eyebrow briefly rise and fall. "Could you be a dear and change the reservation?"

Kelli doesn't need to ask where. Every year they go to Sorriento's. It was her father's favorite restaurant.

***

Kelli leans close to the mirror and applies the mascara, her long thin fingers holding the wand, her movements so elegant they remind me of a symphony conductor. She is stunning in a red summer dress, the color accentuating her tan. Setting the mascara aside, she reaches for lipstick and carefully applies it. When she finishes she studies herself critically. I meow my approval as a cat is incapable of a wolf whistle.

"Leonardo, you are such a sweet kitty," she tells me as she reaches to pet me. I move my head against her hand and purr my love to her. She picks me up carefully, holding me away from her so as not to get hair on her dress, and sets me on the bathroom sink. I look at myself in the mirror. Quite dashing, if I do say so.

"Pray, Leonardo," she says seriously. "Pray for my dad, who died ten years ago today. Pray that his soul rests in peace. Pray for my mom, that she also finds peace and that tonight her dominant emotion will be happiness." She strokes my cheeks with her thumbs and looks into my eyes. "And pray for me. Pray that I'm making the right decision and that I find the right words to tell Mom."

I look at her curiously. Tell her what? What decision? I feel a knot in my tummy.

She checks her wristwatch and stands. "Be a good boy, Leonardo," she tells me as she leaves the bathroom and starts down the stairs.

Of course, I follow. I know she doesn't want me to leave the house but I must. There is a screen loose in her mother's bedroom that I push through to the porch roof. From there it's an easy leap to the tree limb where I wait as she passes by. When she is a safe distance ahead, I scamper down the tree and pick my way down the street, scurrying beneath parked cars, weaving around trees and keeping her in my sight but me out of hers.

It's not a long walk. Three streets down and two over from her home, she stops outside a door and checks her wristwatch before rubbing her hands together nervously. I cautiously move closer until I am just three parked cars away. I watch as she turns her head, checking the sidewalk in both directions and it occurs to me that she is looking for her mom.

A car horn startles me and I see Kelli look, smile, and wave. A few moments later I hear footsteps on the pavement and see Kelli embracing someone. As she turns around I see that it's not her mom. No, it's a man. He's a few inches taller than she, with an athletic build and curly black hair. He is smiling, and has a nice smile with perfect teeth. His skin is tan like Kelli's, only more so. He reminds me of someone and I am still trying to recall who when they open the door to the establishment and go inside.

The aromas from the open door float toward me on the light summer breeze and I feel a rumbling in my stomach. I start to leave my hiding place for one closer to the door when I catch a familiar scent: the perfume worn by Mrs. Parker. I sit still and watch as she walks past quickly, her lips pressed firmly together, her brow pinched.

When she enters, I make my move. I run full speed to the side of the building, then move to the full glass door and peer in. I see Mrs. Parker following a man in a tuxedo toward the back.

Fortunately, this building is the first of a row of connecting buildings and I have no trouble moving alongside it to the back. Though the aromas from the kitchen are divine, my focus is listening, not eating, so I scour the area for a vantage point, but see nothing useful. Then it occurs to me that maybe I'm looking in the wrong place.

I'm up to the roof in a hop, skip, and a jump. Literally. I hop to the top of the dumpster, skip to the top of the stacked crates, then jump to the roof. The tar on the roof is hot and sticky so I look quickly about, finding my mark. There's a large skylight in the center, the perfect place to watch—and hopefully listen.

I find a shaded spot between the skylight and a vent where the tar is cool, and crouch, looking through the glass until I see them. Voices drift upward through the vent to the warm night air where my ears gather them in and try to disentangle the menagerie. I focus, adjusting my ears independently to and fro until at last I pick up familiar voices.

"Mom, Nabil has been accepted into the Masters program at UCLA."

"Congratulations, Nabil. Which program?

"Thank you, Mrs. Parker," he says as he places the napkin on his lap. "I hope to direct movies so I am entering the Film and Television program."

"My, how exciting," Mrs. Parker says, though, if you ask me, her voice lacks enthusiasm.

The waiter interrupts the conversation and, after the order is placed, their interaction drags. Kelli rearranges her silverware, Mrs. Parker stares at her plate, and Nabil glances around the room. Kelli and Nabil exchange a look and I see her nod her head slightly.

"Mom, I—I mean *we*, have something to tell you," Kelli says in a voice so quiet I can barely pick it out.

Mrs. Parker looks up and I can see her stiffen. She opens her mouth as if to speak, then closes it and nods her head.

I jump and scurry for safety at the sound of a truck backfiring. When I regain my composure, Nabil sits alone at the table. Catching a glimpse of Kelli hurrying toward the front of the restaurant, I scamper across the rooftop, leaping onto the ledge. I peer down and see Mrs. Parker pacing briskly in front of the restaurant. The door swings open and Kelli rushes out and yells, "Mom."

Mrs. Parker stops pacing, her back to her daughter. Fumbling with her purse as Kelli slowly walks toward her, she extracts a handkerchief and dabs at her eyes. Her shoulders sag and Kelli reaches out to her and gently touches her back just below her hair, between her shoulder blades.

"Mom, are you okay?" Kelli asks softly, her voice almost lost in the din of the busy street.

Mrs. Parker nods but does not turn around.

Kelli moves closer and wraps her arms around her mom, her chin resting on the older woman's shoulder. "Talk to me, Mom. Please," Kelli pleads.

Mrs. Parker turns to look at Kelli, taking her daughter's face in her hands. "This news was just so sudden and unexpected," she starts. "I'm sorry if I embarrassed you but I was just so overcome with emotion."

"Mom, I'm sorry," Kelli says, but Mrs. Parker placed her finger on Kelli's lips.

"I just wish your father could be here to see what a wonderful woman our daughter has become." She leans in and kisses Kelli's cheek before whispering in her ear, "And now I have two reasons to celebrate this day. Your birthday and your engagement."

Life Nine ~ Exodus

June, 2199

Fat drops of rain hit the pavement and I dart into the doorway of an abandoned building to avoid being struck. This is acid rain; it singed my fur recently when I was unlucky enough not to find shelter quickly. We all know that acid rain has been around for centuries, but with the massive amounts of carbon dioxide in the air in the past few years, the trapped gasses have combined with the moisture in the atmosphere to form a highly toxic mixture of sulfuric and nitric acids: the dreadful precipitation that we now call mega-acid rain. I can actually see steam rising from the drops and the odor of sulfur permeates the air, making it difficult to breath and stinging my nostrils and eyes. I hate it.

This type of rainfall is becoming more frequent, and, when it occurs, the result is disastrous to every living thing on the planet. Only the largest and sturdiest trees have survived and even those are leafless, their trunks and branches scarred. It's obvious that they, too, will soon succumb. The buildings are also pitted and scored; some of the older ones have already begun to collapse in upon themselves and I must be very careful to avoid being struck by chunks of falling concrete and rusted metal. Only if driven by extreme hunger do I venture into those areas to hunt the mice that still dwell within their walls.

This is my final life and, I am sad to say, the final days of the world as we know it. I wasn't aware until this, my ninth life, that I have been upon this earth eight other times. When you see a cat with the wisdom of the ages in his or her eyes, you are no doubt looking at one of us who has reached this final chapter in the book of lives, the final life in which we become not only self-aware and conscious of our own mortality, but also cognizant of our past lives. It has had a profound effect upon me.

My thoughts have often turned back in time and I have recounted each life that I have lived, and the humans that I have loved, with an equal mixture of joy and melancholy. I wish I could have done something to affect the heartrending fate of some, but I know that is impossible. I think with longing of being held and feeling protected in the arms of the humans who loved me and who I loved in return.

But enough of this looking into the distant past; I must focus on the situation at hand. For, you see, the earth is dying from too many years of abuse, of chemicals being dumped into the oceans, lakes, and rivers. From too many years of burying non-biodegradable material deep with the ground, making it barren for centuries to come. And from too many years of spewing noxious fumes and gases into the atmosphere and disregarding the melting of the polar icecaps. All of the warnings were ignored. Until now. Until it is too late. The days of reckoning are upon us.

To further explain the events that are unfolding and my place in them I should digress just a bit; not to the distant past, but to a bit earlier in my current life. My name is Frankie and I am of the Abyssinian breed, one dating back to the days of the Egyptian pharaohs, so I feel as though in a way I have indeed come full circle. People have commented on my regal bearing and exclaim over my silky tabby-colored fawn coat. They seem especially taken with my "dramatic" facial markings that are in a darker hue of sepia, but I try not to read too much into their accolades.

I have resided with my humans since I was a kitten and quickly developed a strong bond of affection with Professor Charles Sidwell, but am sorry to say that I've never achieved that same warm relationship with his wife, Pricilla—or Prissy, as both friends and foes alike call her. I am unhappily numbered amongst the latter group as she doesn't like animals in general and me in particular. I can't agree more that her nickname fits her. She is a shallow, ill-tempered woman and I must admit that I have no idea what the professor sees in her.

I've always thought of the professor as a man of great knowledge and wisdom. He was one of the world's foremost authorities on the affects of global warming and foresaw that it would lead to catastrophic events. My soul now weeps as I look at the surrounding devastation and see that he was correct in all that he stated. Some enlightened folk called him the new Nostradamus, able to foretell the future of our planet much as the ancient soothsayer had predicted events far in advance of his own lifetime. I don't know about all of that, but I do know that the professor often remarked that "The earth has grown mightily sick of us humans and the day will come, not too far in the future, I fear, when she will finally destroy the blight that is upon her, which is humanity." I would always rub my head against his leg when he said that, and he would reach down to give me a quick scratch behind my ears and a pat before returning to his ponderings.

Alas, some of those events are happening now. From what I understand, the climate system has become extremely unstable. At the beginning of the century the rapid rising of the sea levels caused the major coastal cities of L.A., Rio, Sao Paulo, Bombay, Tokyo, Kobe, London, and Shanghai to be flooded to the extent that they are now below sea level. When that happened, the professor explained to me that the various governments of the world told the millions of people that had to evacuate their homes not to worry, that the water would eventually recede and the great cities would be rebuilt, this is just an ordinary cycle of the weather and soon all would return to normal.

The professor had snorted and declared that things would never return to normal. And apparently he was right. Over the next decade, the sea levels continued to expand, the mountain glaciers melted as did the Greenland Ice Sheet. El Nino came more frequently and the first Category 6 Hurricane developed, destroying the coastal areas of Louisiana and Florida and spawning multiple vicious F5 tornadoes that ripped across the south and mid-west. In a matter of weeks, cities too numerous to count were reduced to mere rubble. The states of Kansas and Oklahoma were the hardest hit, with not a single major city left whole in the aftermath. I shivered as I imagined the destruction that Mother Nature had unleashed upon the earth.

Too afraid to live above ground, people built homes beneath the surface, venturing out less and less as the conditions above continued to deteriorate. Whole subterranean cities were built, but even these were in danger as earthquakes became more and more frequent. In addition, newly discovered underground volcanoes were beginning to show signs of eruption. I heard it said repeatedly that the end was near; we just didn't know when the final death blow would be dealt. There was rapidly becoming no safe place on earth to go.

It was finally realized that something drastic had to be done if mankind was to survive. It was too late to stop the devastation of this planet so they did the only thing they could: they looked for another place to live. A multi-national effort comprised of the wealthiest and most advanced countries had been in the works for thirty years to relocate the inhabitants of Earth to another planet. In 2155, a planet had been discovered by Herbert Johansson. It had gone unnoticed until then as its trajectory around the sun was parallel to Earth's. Many trips were made to obtain water and soil samples for testing, and once it had been determined that the planet could sustain life, plans for the eventual exodus from Earth to the new Promised Land were made. The new planet was named Eden.

The Sidwells were wealthy people, so the professor and Prissy were able to book passage upon one of the transportation crafts, the Arks, named after the great ship that was built during the flooding of the earth. He arranged my passage on one of the cargo ships taking livestock and other creatures to the new world. I was grateful that he thought to include me; I knew that a lot of others were not as fortunate. Prissy had sniffed and complained about the cost of my fare but the professor was adamant.

"Frankie is part of this family and will go with us to the new world," he told her and refused to discuss it anymore. I was as surprised as she that he had taken this stand against her wishes. He rarely stood up to her, being a kind and gentle soul who only wanted to read his books and study the environment.

We were to depart within two weeks and all was a flurry of activity as bags were packed and decisions were made as to what to take. There was only so much space allocated to each traveler. Then, without warning, everything changed. I was sitting in the study watching as the professor methodically packed some of his most prized books to take to Eden. I could feel that something was wrong and I was very anxious. Suddenly he grabbed his chest, let out a tiny gasp, and fell to the floor. I cried out and ran to him, nudging his arm and trying to awaken him. An instant later, Prissy ran into the room and shooed me roughly away. Not much later I saw men come and take him away. The next day Prissy returned home; one look at her tear-stained face confirmed the worst: the professor was dead. I overhead her telling a man to pack up all of his belongings and remove them, that she couldn't bear to look at them now that he was gone. I mourned him greatly.

My life changed after that, and not for the better. Prissy, as I've mentioned, didn't much care for me and although I tried to stay out of her way, my very presence seemed to annoy her. I often found myself begging meals from the few neighbors that were left to survive.

Then the day came for us to leave. A terrible storm had struck the night before and the air was sharp with the scent of acid rain. I was glad that I was leaving this horrible place. When the driver came to pick us up, Prissy looked down at me and shook her head.

"I'm not taking that creature with me," she stated matter-of-factly. "I know my husband was quite fond of it, but I can't abide it. Please take it somewhere and dispose of it." With that, she entered the vehicle without a backwards glance. The man made a grab for me but I feinted to one side and scrambled past him. The house was near the entrance to the outside so I ran in that direction. The great doors were open, and I darted through them.

Over the next several months I learned to fend for myself, eking out a bleak existence on garbage and the occasional rodent too old or sick to avoid my amateur attempts at hunting. After a while, my once silky fur was dull and rough, and my ribs protruded. I was slowly starving to death. Then something happened that changed my life forever. I had killed a large mouse. To this day I'm still not sure how I managed that in my weakened condition. As I was getting ready to feast upon my good fortune, I heard a low growl nearby and suddenly a large calico cat pounced upon me, viciously clawing and biting me. When I tried to defend myself it grabbed the mouse and leapt toward the door. Knowing that I would most likely die without this food, I flung myself upon my attacker and began slashing with my back claws and biting as hard as I could. I was no match for my larger foe, but still I continued to fight until I lay panting and exhausted. With a final growl, the cat picked up the mouse and stalked toward the open door. There it paused and gave me a final disdainful glare as it turned to leave.

Suddenly an even larger cat, black as the night, blocked its escape. Spitting and hissing, the calico dropped my mouse and leapt on the black cat. The black cat struck back with truly awe inspiring swiftness and ferocity that sent the other cat fleeing. He picked up the mouse in his mouth and, to my surprise and dread, began to walk slowly toward me. I cringed and pushed myself further into a dark corner. Stopping before me, the black cat eyed me for a long moment and then dropped the mouse at my feet. I crouched, frozen with fear, unable to move. With a sigh the cat pushed the mouse toward me. Cautiously, I reached out and patted the mouse with a paw, keeping a wary eye upon the beast that now sat before me. He seemed to nod his head in encouragement. Finally, my desperate hunger overcame my fear and I began to devour my hard-earned meal. The black cat seemed content to merely sit and watch.

With my stomach full for the first time in many weeks, I was unable to stave off sleep. When I awoke the cat was stretched out next to me, his massive head leaning slightly against my side. I stared at him, noting that in addition to a partially missing left ear, he had several small scars on his face. Then he opened his eyes, blinked sleepily, and yawned, showing a mouthful of impressive fangs. To my amazement, I felt comforted by his presence instead of afraid, even though I knew that one swat of his mighty paw would surely be the end of me.

So occurred another turning point in my life. Midnight, as I learned he was named by the humans with whom he once lived, taught me how to better stalk the mice that dwelled in the abandoned building that I now called home. Of course, with his vast experience and greater size, he was much more proficient at it than I and usually it was he who ended up sharing his meal with me. I have no idea why he decided to take me under his wing, but I was grateful. The days passed and, except for the rumblings of the earth, which were becoming more constant, they were peaceful. We hunted. We ate. We slept. I gained weight and my coat was once again soft and silky.

We sometimes sat and observed the humans as they left on their journey to Eden. The more violent storms have nearly abated and the ships are now arriving at the docking station and leaving at a more rapid pace. It seems as though a new sense of urgency has possessed them and this disquiets me. I wish the professor were here to tell me what was going on. I glance at Midnight and can tell that he, too, is uneasy.

More and more often we crept nearer to the docking stations and watched.

The people avoid making eye contact with each other and I can see their wariness and fear as they hurried toward the landing sites. I finally understand. Time is running out and not everyone will be leaving for the land of hope and promise. I learn from snippets of conversations that only the strongest, the brightest, and the wealthiest have so far been granted passage. Livestock, to provide food for the humans, and a variety of domesticated animals like dogs and cats, have been transported to the new world already. Not our kind, though. Not the abandoned pets and half-wild feral cats that roam the ruined cities. No, we will remain here, awaiting the final destruction of Earth.

One day while Midnight was off on his own hunting I heard a commotion at the docking station and drew nearer to watch. Men yelled in the distance and I saw one knocked to the ground and struck about the head by two of the soldiers who guarded the landing sites. He was beaten for several minutes before, finally tiring of their game, the soldiers allowed him to get to his feet. With a final shove that sent him sprawling back onto the asphalt, they let him go on his way. I watched as he staggered, obviously disoriented, his bloodied head cradled in his hands. I have seen many terrible things that humans have done to each other in my many lives and one would think their actions would no longer affect me, but this did. I felt sorry for the man, who obviously wasn't brilliant enough, strong enough, or wealthy enough to gain passage aboard one of the spacecraft. He, like me, was one of the doomed.

A loud rumble deep within Earth's core warned of yet another earthquake and I ran swiftly away from the sound. In mid-flight I looked behind me just in time to see the beaten man stumble and then silently fall into the chasm that opened up beneath him.

The soldiers shouted into their hand-held radios and the spacecraft ceased its descent and hovered about five hundred yards above the landing site. People waiting to board cried out in protest, but the pilots would not risk any damage to the craft. Suddenly fire belched upward from the earth's core and molten lava began to bubble to the surface and run in thin rivulets toward the crowded docking station.

A large land transport vehicle jerked to a halt and, with much pushing and shoving, the passengers scrambled aboard and it lumbered off. A horrendous explosion sounded and I looked over my shoulder and saw the vehicle be flung violently upward and then crash back down to earth as a fireball. I dodged smaller pieces of red-hot metal, still on fire, as they struck the ground around me. I heard no screams from those within the transport, so I knew that their deaths had come mercifully swift, without awareness.

I jumped and hissed as a piece of the falling metal landed on my back and the stench of burning hair reached my nostrils. Panic surged through me as I realized it was my fur that was on fire and I flung myself into the water-filled ditch, hoping that the acid rain had been diluted enough by the more recent flooding. That cats hate water is common knowledge, but let me say with certainty that we hate fire even more. I sighed with relief as the tepid water doused the flames. I climbed out of the ditch, wet and bedraggled, then shook myself to get rid of at least some of the water. The lava had now reached the platform and I watched as the spacecraft accelerated away … no need for it to remain since all of the passengers were now incinerated.

As I returned to the abandoned building that I now called home I saw a figure standing in the shadows. Contact with humans is something that I now avoid but I was drawn to this one for some inexplicable reason. Cautiously I drew nearer, not stopping until I was only a few feet away from the woman. I could see from the guileless look in her eyes and her gentle features that she would do me no harm. But it was even more than that—

"Hello, kitty."

Her voice was soft and melodic as she reached out and stroked my fur with a grubby hand. I didn't move away, but instead leaned into her caress and began to purr as a feeling of contentment welled up inside me. Out of the corner of one eye I saw Midnight hovering nearby and I called to him to join us, but he remained crouched beside some rubble of bricks and steel, watching us. I could tell that he was confused by my actions but I didn't know how to convey to him what was happening in terms that he would understand. You see, I've been looking for this human for a very, very long time.

The woman picked me up and rubbed her face against my fur. She then hugged me so tightly that I thought my ribs would pop right through my skin, but I made no attempt to scratch her or to escape. When she finally loosened her hold I gratefully took a few deep breaths and then patted her cheek with a paw, which made her giggle.

"You're a pretty kitty. I think I'll name you Kitty Cat. My name is Bekka." She tucked me up under one arm and ambled deeper into the building.

Midnight followed at a distance. We traveled for a long time and then descended a flight of stairs into what used to be a subway station. Once there we navigated a maze of tunnels that sloped gradually downward until we finally reached our destination: a small room containing a single mattress and chair. Humming, the woman set me upon the chair and twirled around the room before coming to a stop directly in front of me.

"This is my home, Kitty Cat. Do you like it?" She scratched my chin and smiled at me. "I was sad to be by myself, but now I have you. And maybe the other kitty, too." With that, she looked at Midnight, who was hovering in the doorway, and held out her hand to him. He didn't come closer but held his ground as she moved toward him. Upon reaching him, she gently stroked his head. Sensing his distrust, she made no attempt to pick him up. "I'll call you Black Kitty," she told him. Finally she moved away and lay down upon the mattress.

I hopped down from the chair and snuggled close to her, feeling very protective. After a few minutes I could tell she was asleep by her deep, rhythmic breathing. I relaxed and slept, too. When I awoke, Midnight was gone and, although I hoped he would come back, I knew that I would stay with the woman whether he did or not.

Bekka stirred in her sleep, making little murmuring sounds, and then rubbed her hands along her stomach. I nuzzled her side and she soon slept peacefully once again. Unblinking, I sat and watched her, thinking of the long road I had traveled to find her. It seemed ironic to me that I had finally found her in this, my last life, my last chance, but, then again, perhaps this was how it was meant to be all along.

I must admit that I thought I had found this soul a couple of times along the way. Two special humans who had loved me as I loved them come to mind: my gentle Falling Rain and my sweet Jingfei. Although neither of them was the one I sought, that didn't make me love them any less.

I heard stealthy footsteps outside the room and I positioned myself between the sleeping woman and the intruder, prepared to defend her with my life. A pair of yellow eyes peered back at me from the darkness and I heaved a sigh of relief as I recognized Midnight. He had returned after all. We curled up together and as he slept I began to try to think of a way to get Bekka onto one of the transport ships that would take her to Eden. It would be a daunting undertaking and perhaps even an impossible one, but I knew that to save this woman was my destiny.

I had to act swiftly as time was quickly running out. The next morning, I made my way to a nearby docking station. I had been watching the transport ships coming and going for the past few months and had noticed a pattern. At each full moon a larger transport ship would arrive and actually remain on the ground for several hours. During this time animals or equipment would be loaded. The next full moon was just a few nights away; I had to find a way to get Bekka onto the spacecraft and find it fast.

I returned to the little room to find Bekka awake and eating some small apples, their skins brown and wrinkled. I wondered if Midnight could catch a mouse for her so she wouldn't have to eat such poor fare.

After she finished, she put on her mismatched shoes and we made our way outside. As Bekka stood looking around I took the hem of her skirt between my teeth and tugged on it. Perplexed, she looked at me then shook a finger at me, telling me to stop. I meowed at her, urging her to follow. Finally, deciding I wanted to play a game, she allowed me to pull her along toward the docking station. Her eyes widened when she realized where I was going and she stopped, refusing to go further.

"No, Kitty Cat. I can't go near where those big things come down. Those nasty men yelled at me and said I was a retard and too stupid to be saved." She shook her head sadly. "They were mean, Kitty Cat. Why did they say that? I know I'm not smart. My daddy used to tell me that, too. But why does being stupid make you not worth saving?"

Unable to voice my opinion that they were the stupid ones, I rubbed against her leg to soothe her. So there we remained and, despite all of my efforts, I could not coax her to go any further. How was I going to get her on the spacecraft? Then Midnight made a strange yowling sound and I was distracted from my dilemma as I went to investigate.

The next three days were frustrating as I tried in vain to get Bekka closer to the docking station. If I couldn't get her to even go near it, there was no hope that I could get her on board the transport ship. Each night after she fell asleep I would slip out. I hated to leave her alone, but most nights I had little choice. I would return to the site and explore it, trying to find a solution. I was beginning to panic. Tonight the moon would be full and the transport ship would arrive shortly after dawn. I had to find a way. I just had to. I hurried back to the little room. Back to the child-like woman whom others thought wasn't worth saving.

Shortly before dawn, I woke her by licking her cheek. Drowsily she looked at me and tried to shoo me away.

"Sleepy, Kitty Cat. I wanna go back to sleep." I redoubled my efforts and began to also tap her face with my paw and meow loudly until, with a groan, she slowly rose to a sitting position. After rubbing her eyes, she focused on me with a frown. "What's wrong, Kitty Cat?" She turned to Midnight and asked, "Black Kitty, do you know what's wrong with Kitty Cat?"

Midnight, having returned just moments earlier, blinked at us and yawned. I nipped at Bekka's ankles and tugged at her skirt as I always did when I wanted her to follow me. Reluctantly, she slipped on her shoes and followed me out into the pre-dawn light. Midnight trailed behind us. I took a circuitous route toward the docking station, zigging and zagging until I was sure that Bekka had no idea where we were going. If luck was with me, we would be nearly upon the site before she realized where we were. If I'd had fingers I would have crossed them.

As we popped out of an alleyway, I saw two soldiers standing a short distance away and beyond them I saw that the transport ship had landed and was systematically being loaded with huge crates and strange looking equipment too large to be boxed.

I darted toward a stack of crates with Bekka close behind me. I had crossed half the distance between the crates and us when I heard her gasp in shock as she saw the two soldiers and obviously realized where she was. Before she could turn and run away, I grabbed a mouthful of her long skirt and pulled her toward the huge boxes of equipment stacked along a wall to the left of the men. Too frightened to resist, Bekka followed my lead and together we stumbled between them and hid.

"Kitty Cat," she whispered, "those are bad men. I wanna go home." I blocked her retreat and tried to force her to move toward the ship. "Kitty Cat, I know what you want." I shot her a surprised look that I'm sure even my cat features conveyed clearly. She reached down and patted my head. "You want Bekka to get on the big ship don't you, Kitty Cat?" Her sudden insight gladdened me, although I wasn't sure what to make of it. I patted her leg in return and tried again to herd her toward the docked ship. "I can't, Kitty Cat. The soldier men will get me." She eyed me solemnly. "They'll get you, too. You can't save me, Kitty Cat." I again vowed that I would die trying.

Just then I saw Midnight trot up to the two soldiers. "Look at that mangy cat," I heard one of the men exclaim. "Ugly bastard."

Midnight hissed and swiped at him with a mighty paw. The man yelped in pain as the razor-like claws penetrated the cloth of the soldier's pants and raked the tender skin beneath it. "Son of a bitch."

Midnight hissed again and sidestepped to avoid the rifle butt the man swung at him. Ears flattened again his huge head, he growled and held his ground.

"Kill it," the other man yelled and laughed.

Midnight growled again, even more menacingly than before, and swatted at them once again, this time striking nothing but air. I watched in fascination and incredulity as he gradually led the two men away from where Bekka and I were hiding. I don't know if he consciously intended to distract the soldiers in order to give us a chance to reach the spacecraft, but that's exactly what happened.

When they began to chase Midnight, I cried softly at Bekka and began tugging on her skirt again. I was greatly relieved when she slowly began to follow me. We wove our way between the crates until we reached the ship's loading dock. Several men had been working to load the ship but they were now moving toward the two soldiers as they cursed and struck at the huge black cat. I heard one of them offer a wager that the cat would win and another take the bet.

I forced myself to ignore them all and concentrated on getting on board the ship. Once I was certain they were all preoccupied, I ran up the ramp and into the interior of the vessel. Bekka crept along the ramp and I cringed, sure the men would see her if she didn't hurry. After what seemed an eternity, she finally reached my side and we moved together further in, looking for a place to hide. Following a narrow pathway between the crates we finally found a slightly wider space against a far wall. Gratefully, Bekka sank down, wrapped her arms around her knees, and rocked back and forth.

I dashed back to the front of the ship and crouched in the wide doorway, watching as Midnight leapt away from the group of men and disappeared into a maze of buildings. Shots rang out as one of the soldiers tried to shoot him as he fled, but I could see the bullets strike the concrete and heaved a sigh of relief. The other men headed back to the ship to continue their work and I returned to Bekka, nuzzling her and licking the tears from her cheeks, trying to comfort her.

It was a few hours later when I heard the men saying that they had only a few more crates to load. I knew that the ship would soon depart. Cautiously I crept once again toward the still-open doorway and peered out. I heard a faint noise and turned toward it. Midnight meowed softly again at me and I bobbed my head in return. I knew he wanted me to join him but I couldn't. I had a job to do. Then, to my amazement, he moved quickly toward me. I scurried backward as he approached so that I could lead him to where Bekka was hiding. I saw his huge head and half-missing ear appear at the top of the loading dock ramp and my heart sang with gladness. He was coming with us.

"Hey." I froze at the man's shout and watched in horror as his booted foot connected solidly with Midnight's ribs. I saw his huge body lift up into the air and heard it land hard upon the concrete with a sickening thud. Then I heard the sharp retort of a rifle followed by the soldier's laughter. "That cat won't be scratching nobody now."

My heart was heavy as I returned to Bekka. She had heard the shot and looked at me with wide, terrified eyes, and I knew that she knew. "Poor Black Kitty," she whispered. Then she began to quietly sob. The engines roared as the ship made ready to depart. I rested my head upon her lap and together we grieved for Midnight.

***

I hadn't known that the trip to Eden would take so long. It had been several days since we left Earth. We survived by stealing scraps of food from the man who patrolled the area in which we hid. But there was very little to drink and I made certain that most of it went to Bekka. Her life was much more important than my own. I realized this even if she did not.

Thirst and hunger made us more reckless as the days passed and then the inevitable happened. Bekka spied a nearly full plate of still-warm pasta and canister of drink sitting on the desk where the watchman often did his paperwork. Despite my meowed warnings that it was too soon, that he might come back, she crept out of hiding and snatched both. The man saw her and ordered her to stop. I could see the terror on her face as she dropped the food and drink and fled.

Unfortunately, she ran down a narrow opening between some crates that ended in a wall. Pressing her back against it, she could do nothing but watch as he came toward her. I darted between his legs and turned to face him with a growl and hiss. The man paused and looked at Bekka speculatively for a long moment then glanced down at me before returning his gaze to her. I saw something flicker in his eyes. Pity?

Then he dropped to one knee and said quietly, "It's okay. I won't hurt you." He reached out a hand and I swatted it away, leaving thin ribbons of blood where my claws had raked his flesh. He jerked his hand back and swore. I felt a small sense of satisfaction that I had at least drawn first blood. Then he did the unexpected and removed a flask from his hip and slid it along the floor toward us.

"Go ahead. Take it," he said to Bekka.

She stared at it but made no move.

"It's just water. I know you must be thirsty." He lowered himself to the floor and crossed his legs, obviously in no hurry to leave. "I've suspected that someone—or something—was hiding up here." He laughed softly. "It was pretty obvious from the missing food that I wasn't alone. That's why I started leaving more of it out. I just didn't realize that I was feeding more than one or I would have left larger portions and more to drink."

Bekka now had the flask and was drinking greedily from it. I stayed where I was, watching the man. His eyes were kind, but I remained wary. I still didn't dare to trust him.

Joe, as he introduced himself, brought us food and drink every day after that. Sometimes he would sit on the floor and talk to us about his life and his family. He said once that Bekka reminded him of his younger sister who had died of leukemia when she was only twelve years old. Other times he would just place our meal on the desk and leave to attend to his other duties. After a time, I began to relax around him and even came to realize that on the days he didn't stay I missed his company. I think Bekka missed it, too.

Finally came the day that I had looked forward to with a combination of longing and apprehension during the past several months of travel. Joe came to us and announced that we were approaching Eden. He told us this was his final trip, so he would be able to stay with us for a while and help us find a place in the new world. Gratitude washed over me at his promise; I hadn't had a plan for that. With a word of warning that we must hide ourselves from everyone but him, he left us to make ready for the landing. Bekka hugged me to her and I could hear the wild thumping of her heart as she giggled with glee. I patted her cheek with my paw and we went to hide until Joe came back for us.

The light of two moons bathed the landscape as we surveyed our new home. Joe had sneaked us out of the spacecraft as soon as it was safe to do so and then brought us to a solitary campsite that he'd made for us far from the landing site. He cautioned that it wasn't safe for us to be among the others until he found Bekka suitable clothing.

Then he shook his head and added, ruefully, perhaps not even then. It was too obvious that she was different. The government on Eden wasn't kind in how it dealt with the few stowaways who had tried to make their way to the new world without proper documentation. They were placed in a cramped holding unit until they could be sent back to Earth. My heart skipped a beat at his words. To have traveled all this distance only to be in harm's way again was almost more than I could bear. But for now, at least, we were safe, with shelter and plenty of food.

Joe had seen to that.

For the next several days we rested and explored by turns the area around our new home. The soil of Eden was a hue of crimson so bright it appeared that the ground bled each time it was dug up. This disturbed me a little. But I found the colors of the flora and fauna beautiful. Most people seemed to think that we animals see only in black and white, or maybe a few shades of gray, but we can see hues and colors as vividly as humans. I enjoyed exploring and hunted small rodent-like creatures which I discovered tasted a great deal like chicken. I was content for the first time in a long while.

Joe traveled under the cover of darkness between the campsite and the city that was constantly under construction as buildings were erected to house the throng of humanity arriving from Earth. He brought Bekka suitable clothing but still refused to take us into the city, saying that it was still too risky. Trusting that Joe was right in his assessment, she and I remained in our little campsite, just the two of us.

"I'm trying to find a doctor we can trust," he told Bekka one evening.

Bekka tilted her head to one side as she always did when thinking and said in a puzzled voice, "Why are you finding a doctor? Are you sick?"

Joe shook his head. "No, it's for you, and we need someone who won't turn you in for being here illegally."

"But I'm not sick, either," she said, still sounding bewildered.

Joe looked at her for a long minute then sighed as he realized that she was serious. Slowly, haltingly, he explained her condition to her while she stared at him in silence. He left a little while later to return to the city, reminding Bekka to rest and eat well. She quietly assured him that she would and remained uncharacteristically subdued long after he had gone.

On a misty morning about two weeks after our arrival, I heard Bekka cry out in pain and I rushed to her side, meowing my concern. She grasped her abdomen and leaned heavily against the table where we took our meals. After a long moment she blew out a breath and sat down shakily.

"Kitty Cat, I don't feel so good. My stomach hurts real bad."

I rubbed against her leg to comfort her. A few minutes later she doubled over again and made little mewling sounds. She looked at me with wide eyes as the pain subsided. I wasn't sure if Bekka understood what was happening to her and I looked around anxiously, wishing without hope that Joe would arrive, but I knew that he wouldn't be back until nightfall. Bekka moved slowly to the cot where she slept and gingerly lowered herself onto it. There she remained for the rest of the day, her cries of pain growing louder with each passing hour. I could do nothing but pace back and forth outside the tent, watching for Joe as the sun finally began to slowly sink in the darkening sky.

An ear-splitting scream made me jump and I yowled in fear. If Joe didn't come soon, I was certain that Bekka would surely die. Then I heard a sound that gladdened my heart and I ran back inside. There atop Bekka's stomach lay a newborn child. A male. His wizened little face scrunched up and his tiny fists flailed against his mother as he wailed. From the strength of his cries it appeared that he was strong and healthy. His mother, in contrast, looked pale and weak; blood was beginning to pool on the floor of the tent beneath her.

Bekka smiled weakly at me and whispered, "Look, Kitty Cat. I got a baby." Her eyes locked with mine then dimmed and she became still. *No.* Heartbroken, I moved closer, but then heard the crunch of hurried footsteps and whirled to face the tent entrance.

Joe burst through the door and I heard his breath catch as he looked at Bekka and her son. He fell to his knees beside them and took her limp hand in his.

"Oh, my God. I'm so sorry, Bekka. I thought there was more time. Time to find you a doctor. But I … I couldn't." He raised his head, eyes bright with unshed tears and looked at the baby. Picking up a knife from the table he carefully cut the umbilical cord that connected mother and child and quickly wrapped the infant in a clean blanket.

I saw the awe and wonder on his face as he looked down at the wriggling bundle in his arms and I knew that he felt it. That he knew as I did that this infant was special.

Extraordinary. Chosen.

Although deeply mourning Bekka, who had passed from this world bringing forth new life, I was also aware of a profound sense of hope and purpose coursing through me. This child, although I knew not how, would be the salvation of us all. And I knew that Joe and I would be by his side.

His companions.

His guardians.

His disciples.

Epilogue

I am weary.

Longer is the time I spend sleeping before the fire, dreaming dreams of lives past and loved ones lost. They were shrouded once, hidden from my consciousness until this final life … but they are clear to me now and growing ever closer.

They comfort me.

Gentle hands stroke me, smoothing my fur and easing—at least for a little while—the aching pains in my aged body. I hear the boy murmuring words of endearment and open my eyes to gaze upon his face, wishing I could lessen the sadness I see upon it. He smiles at me and then leans down to nuzzle my face with his. I realize quite suddenly that he is really no longer a boy.

Many years have passed since the birth of Bekka's son Jacob. Joe and I have guarded him well these past sixteen years, filled with tranquility at times, but mostly with great trepidation. We have survived myriad changes to the government on this new planet we now call home. Changes that were as often as not the result of wars over boundaries and usurpation of power that were followed by brief times of peace Then the cycle of conflict would begin again. It reminds me yet of an old Chinese curse that Joe would sometimes utter when things were at their worst: "May you live in interesting times."

Jacob gives my head a final pat and begins his daily chores. I watch him, pride and love warming me as even the fire burning cheerfully in the fireplace cannot. He will be the greatest of leaders, giving hope where there is hopelessness and bringing a final peace in the midst of recurrent warfare, joining mankind together in unity as never before.

This is his destiny.

I only regret that I will not be there to celebrate his greatest triumphs or share his greatest sorrows. He must continue his journey without me. I know that I am dying. It is the natural order of the universe that for every beginning there is an end.

I have traveled many miles and seen many things during my time in this world and I long for the eternal peace my heart tells me I will find beyond this life. I know not for certain what will happen when I cross over into the realm of final death; surely no one can.

If I had this knowledge between my many incarnations, it was not carried into each new life, yet I *believe*. I believe that somehow I will be joined with the Creator, the maker of all things, and that joining will be wondrous.

Sleep tugs insistently and I feel it covering me, soft and warm as a woolen cloak. My pain subsides and I willingly succumb. Lazily I drift along in the arms of peaceful slumber, lightly at first, then deeper and deeper still.

"Kitty Cat."

My ear twitches and I angle it toward the sound, not much more than a whisper.

"Kitty Cat." Again, softly as before.

With great difficulty I raise my head and look around, seeing only shadows in the darkness. I begin to close my eyes again when a movement catches my attention: a silhouette of light. An apparition? A phantom of mere light and shadow?

And then I see more clearly. It is her.

"Hello, Kitty Cat."

She walks toward me until her outstretched hand reaches my head and she lays it gently upon me. Bekka smiles. It is radiant yet tranquil, and I want only to bask in it for eternity. In a literal blink of an eye I find myself in her lap, on the floor next to the fireplace. All is luminous, glowing with a light that surrounds us. She is dressed in a flowing gown of white satin, her chocolate brown hair falling in a shiny curtain down her back. I look into her eyes and see she no longer suffers any afflictions as she did in life. I see no evidence of the child-like woman she once was.

Am I dead? Am I going to the Creator now?

"No, Kitty Cat, you have not yet passed from this realm into the next."

You can hear my thoughts?

"Yes, dearest one." Burying her face in my fur she hugs me tightly and when she raises her head I see the glisten of tears in her eyes … joyful tears, I think.

"Thank you, Kitty Cat. Thank you for staying with my son when I could not. Joe is a good man, strong and true, but he couldn't have done it alone. He needed you. They both needed you."

I look at her, humbled by her gratitude. I am but a cat.

Stroking my head gently, she continues, "You have touched many lives with much devotion and selflessness, so I have come with a gift for you. You may visit each of your human companions so they may speak with you and tell you what you meant to them. Listen to their voices and hear their stories, Kitty Cat. Walk with them and you will know all that you wish to know."

***

My ears perk at the sound of another voice. Somewhere over … the sound of singing. A beautiful voice floats to me, filling me with joy. I know that voice. Yes, yes, I am certain now. It is Yunet.

She smiles and motions to me. "Come, Tumaini. Come closer so I may touch you."

I run to her and she kneels to greet me. I stand on my hind legs and lick at her face. She laughs as she strokes my back. "I have missed you, too," she tells me.

She cocks her head to one side as if listening to something only she can hear, then nods once. She scratches me behind my ears and gives me a quick hug before rising to her feet.

"Come with me."

Radiant light, dazzling in its intensity, fills me as I step forward. Blinking, my eyes adjust and I slowly gain the ability to make out my surroundings. Vague shapes begin to sharpen with definition until at last I find myself walking along the banks of a mighty river. It looks—no, it *feels* familiar.

For many steps we walk in silence along the great river before my curiosity forces me to wonder where we are going.

"You have a journey to complete, Tumaini, and I will guide you on this first part," Yunet answers. She can hear my thoughts just like Bekka.

She nods at me in acknowledgement.

As we walk, she sings a melody. Her voice floats like fluffy clouds across a blue sky, reminding me of our previous life together. The Nile, Bubastis, the festival of Bast, Kafele. Kafele. Immediately I am filled with grief.

"Don't be sad for Kafele, Tumaini. He is in the house of the Creator and soon we will all be together," Yunet says, ending her song.

Did I not cause his death?

"No, sweet Tumaini. Fanaticism caused his death. Rules, unyielding and without regard to intent, made by man, enforced by those without forgiveness in their hearts. That is what took Kafele's life. You were not aware, but you were a comfort to me as I mourned him, even as you were a comfort to me throughout my life."

She stops and I look at her. "This is where my part of your journey ends." She turns and fades into the light.

***

I'm temporarily disoriented. I rub my eyes and, when I look up, Fatima reaches out to stroke my head. At her touch I feel her serenity and understand that she is at peace. My heart soars to know that this is so. She was a kind and gentle soul who brought much happiness to her father and those who knew her.

"Welcome."

We walk along the streets of Jerusalem, a place to which I vowed never to return, and I'm relieved to see there is no blood upon them now. She tells me of the changes within the great city since the exodus of so many people from Earth to the new world, leaving behind those too poor or imperfect to leave. With bowed head, Fatima says she remains to watch over the souls who cannot fend for themselves. I am puzzled at first when she stops beside a large well, then I realize that it resides on the site of the cellar where she had taken refuge when the Christian soldiers had taken the city. The cellar in which she drew her last breath.

She tells me that the people call her the *Lady of the Well* and often seek her guidance with whispered entreaties, or sometimes simply lay down to sleep peacefully nearby, certain they will be safe under her protection.

Do you not desire to go to the house of the Creator?

"Yes, gentle one. And some day I will, but not yet can I leave this place. The Earth has not been destroyed, although I know that day is soon upon it. There is still much work to be done and I am well content to remain until there are no souls left who need me." She smiles at me. "I wish to tell you how much our time together meant to me and I am sorry that it ended so soon. There was terrible injustice done in this holiest of cities, but there was goodness and purity as well. You helped me hold on to that by simply being a creature that asked nothing except to be treated kindly." She pauses and I follow her gaze to a woman dressed in tattered garments standing hesitantly before the well.

"I must go now. I am needed. Fare thee well."

***

My vision grows darker until only a pinpoint of light exists. I stare at it, mesmerized as it expands outward until I'm blinded by an intense whiteness. I squeeze my eyes close and mew. As I slowly open them, the smell of spring flowers permeates the air and I hear the gurgle of the river nearby. "Do you remember this place?" Gretchen asks and immediately I begin to purr.

"It's good to see you, Familiar," she says to me and I realize that in this life a human never bestowed a name upon me.

Did you suffer greatly?

"Briefly." She leans down and lifts me into her arms and I rub my head under her chin.

I succumbed almost immediately.

She kisses me and whispers, "The suffering will not be brief for those who harmed us."

Silently she carries me down Mount Merkur to the bridge over Oos where we stop and listen to the melodic sounds of this life-sustaining gift. "You were the only one there for me, at the end. The only one who believed I was not evil. Thank you."

I nuzzle against her and knowledge of what she brought to the world fills me. *You became a role model in medicine, an advocate for knowledge over superstition, and, though it came centuries later, a model for women's rights.*

She smiles. "You flatter me, familiar. I was forgotten long before those times."

Your name, but not your actions. Your actions became legend.

She turns her head as if listening to a voice I cannot hear and nods once. She rubs her cheek against mine, tickling my whiskers and sets me on the bridge. "Godspeed, Familiar."

***

I hear the merry tinkle of a bell behind me and turn toward it expectantly.

"Belle, I have missed you." Victoria smiles at me and takes me into her arms. I rub my head against her cheek. "Our time together is short and there is much to say." She is dressed in an elegant gown of pale yellow topped by a fur lined cloak of darkest midnight blue, her golden hair swept up and gathered at the nape of her neck. Pearl earrings dangle delicately from her ears. She is breathtaking.

I take in the winter scene of this little English town where I spent so many happy days, snowflakes drifting down to rest upon the eves of the houses and the boughs of the pines. I draw a deep breath of the brisk air. It feels like heaven.

We stroll along the lane until we reach a grand house. "We moved to this house shortly after you left us, Belle. This is where Andrew and I lived until the end of our days."

Victoria speaks to me of how she and Andrew opened their home to children with disabilities, children that no one wanted. They provided for them and loved them and changed their lives forever.

"People said we were generous—and some said we were a little insane for taking in so many children. But you see, Belle, it was the children that made *our* lives so rich and full. We were blessed to have them and I wouldn't change a single minute of it. And you, my mischievous friend, made it all possible the day you *introduced* me to Andrew. He is my heart and soul, as I am his. Thank you for all of the joy you brought us."

Victoria gently rubs my chin then sets me upon the ground. I watch as she steps away and begins to fade. I see Andrew standing beside her. She leans affectionately against him and I know they will remain together forever.

***

The dusty, sweet scent of the plains grass of the Dakotas draws me and I turn toward it. I hear the beating of drums and the chanting of the Ghost Dance upon the wind. I shiver before I feel hands gently lifting me. I am surprised to see Kicking Bird. I had expected to find Falling Rain standing before me.

He smiles briefly at my bewilderment and ruffles my fur with a calloused palm.

"I know you thought to see Falling Rain, but I have a need to speak with you." He stares out across the plains and as a faraway look comes into his eyes I can see through them to where the buffalo once grazed by the thousands. Suddenly he winces in pain and I know he is seeing the carnage at Wounded Knee. I too, can see it. The booming of cannons shatters the quiet and the coppery scent of blood fills the air. I nearly gag. I force myself not to run away, to remain steadfast.

Kicking Bird sighs and looks at me with sadness. "It is difficult to speak of that day—there is much pain, much sorrow." He hesitates, then touches his hand to his chest. "Here. There is too much pain here in my heart." A slight breeze rises and carries away the smell of blood and death, but it cannot carry away the ache that is also in my heart.

I was not with Falling Rain when she needed me most. I was not by her side at the end. I should have died that day, too.

"You could not help Falling Rain or any of us. It was our destiny to die that day, not yours. Cat, you bore witness to our tragedy and you took part of us with you when the white man took you from this place. You did not realize that every time he looked at you he remembered that day and was ashamed of the atrocity his people perpetrated upon the Lakota people. That is why he kept you with him those many years, not just as a companion to ease his loneliness, but as a constant reminder of what took place. You kept our spirits alive within this white man and in turn he carried our tale to others of his kind so that we would not be forgotten by them."

I see now that he holds a paper in his slightly trembling hands. Slowly, with great deliberation, he reads the newspaper article to me. It recounts in great detail the horror of the senseless slaughter of over three hundred Lakota by the United States Calvary on a bitter cold day in December, 1890. It was written by Sergeant Reginald Armstrong, 7th Calvary Division, and dated December 29, 1910, the twentieth anniversary of the massacre at Wounded Knee.

Folding the paper, he places it inside his ceremonial vest so that it lay against his heart. "Our people suffered much. We are grateful that you kept our story alive within the white man. It means that perhaps we did not die in vain. I am grateful to you." He bows his head to me then raises his eyes to look out at the plains again. That one swift gesture means more than words can express. I am sorry when he begins to walk away. I know he is leaving.

Then he stops and turns back to me. "But I am forgetting something." Smiling, he beckons at something behind me.

"My kitty!"

With joy I leap into the waiting arms of Falling Rain. She giggles and we play, enjoying the simple pleasure of running and jumping; a young girl and her kitten. Yes, I feel like a kitten again. Too quickly, I knew it must, the time has now come when Falling Rain must leave. Solemnly, she bends down and kisses the top of my head and strokes my tail before putting her small hand into Kicking Bird's much larger one. As they enter the brilliant light, she pulls her hand free and steps back to give me a little wave. She is gone.

***

I hear a swoosh, thunk. Swoosh, thunk. The sound ceases and I know that he is standing next to me. He chuckles and reaches down to scratch behind my ears.

Using his walking stick as a brace and bending at the waist, he takes the corner of his garment and dangles it before me. I cannot resist the game. I snag it with my claws and he laughs as he pulls me in a circle. He twirls me a few times before slowing and gently lets me tumble in the grass. He stands up and peers into the distance. "Come, little one."

We are on a dusty road. In the distance I can smell the ocean. He walks briskly and it occurs to me that this Holy Man spent much of his life walking, walking from place to place, helping those in need, teaching love, self-respect, and forgiveness as a way to attain freedom.

Remembering that after his death his nation divided along religious lines and subsequently fought several wars, I couldn't resist feeling that his death had been in vain.

"Really? Is that what you think?" He looks at me as we continue to walk. "Because that's not the truth. Yes, there were horrific wars, genocides, and crimes against humanity, many committed in the name of the Creator. Such sacrilege. But ultimately, at the right time and with the right leader, mankind—" We come to a hilltop overlooking the ocean and he stops. He gazes out over the water, smiling. "Goodbye, my friend."

***

The darkest night and brightest day flash before me in two blinks of an eye and my head feels light. I shake it, trying to regain my balance.

"Are you okay, Qingling?"

I look into the concerned face of Jingfei, squatting down to look at me. *Oh, precious child, I have missed you so.* I place my paws beside her face and lick her cheek.

"I have missed you, too, Qingling," she giggles, embracing, then releasing, me. "Will you walk with me?"

Of course I will.

We walk for a moment in silence. *I failed you. I left you the night they came for you. Will you forgive me?*

"You didn't fail me, Qingling. Our leaders failed me. They failed to protect me from misguided zealots, instead choosing to use them for political gain." She smiles at me. "You were always there for me and I never forgot you."

As we walk through the city streets, Jingfei tells me about her life after our time together. How her father was imprisoned for many years, being released only as an old man near death. "At least we were with him when the spirits came for him," she tells me. Her mother, forced to work in a factory until she was very old, died soon after her father. "I became a teacher," she says, grinning. "Just like my father. And," she adds mischievously, "I taught every student about the Four Olds."

When we cross the Chaobai River at a footbridge, she kneels beside me. "It's been so good talking with you, Qingling." She runs the tip of her index finger down my nose, between my eyes and ears and down the back of my head, causing me to purr. "Goodbye."

She steps from the bridge, disappearing over the water.

***

I hear something splash in the river nearby and fear that Qingling has fallen into the Chaobai. I cry out.

"Leonardo."

The voice is not Qingling's but I instantly recognize it. I run toward the sound. *Kelli.*

She laughs and runs and I chase her, stretching my legs into a lope until I catch her. I leap into the air, landing on her back and she falls, laughing and pulling me on top of her. I lick her face and she holds me tightly. We revel in the moment until finally she sits up and says, "It's so good to see you, Leonardo. Come, walk with me."

The street is familiar. We walk down the sidewalk, the people around us oblivious to our presence. We cross at a corner, a church on one side, a mosque on the other, continuing two more blocks until she stops in front of a two-story brick home with a porch swing that I immediately recognize. An older woman sits in the middle, a young boy and girl on either side. I can see Kelli in the faces of her children as well as in the face of her mother. Kelli watches them smiling. "This is your Grandpa," I hear the woman say showing the children the photos, "and the kitten he is holding is Leonardo."

The door opens and a dark skinned man appears with a tray of cookies and lemonade. *Our hearts are meant to love and forgive.*

I turn to look at Kelli and her face is radiant with love as she fades back into the light.

***

Inexplicably, I feel a sense of urgency, as if I need to be somewhere, somewhere far from here. My step is lively as I walk briskly, pulled along a well-worn path by an irresistible force.

Hurry!

Go faster!

Soon I am running.

Abruptly, the path veers sharply to my left and I follow it through a final line of trees where it opens into a beautiful summer meadow through which a river flows gently. I realize that it is the River of Life and I stare at it in awe. I'm filled with a sense of peace and joy as I step forward, marveling at the sheer beauty and splendor of it all.

Bekka stands before me once more, resplendent in her gown of flowing white.

"Do you understand now, Kitty Cat, how you impacted the lives of those you met along your own journeys of life and death?"

Yes, I understand now. I had purpose.

"Every life, every being, has purpose. All creatures have purpose. This is the true meaning of life, isn't it?" She laughs and the sound is pure and clear. "You mattered, Kitty Cat. You matter still."

I am filled with great emotion and close my eyes. When I open them again I see that Bekka is kneeling next to me with a slender hand outstretched but not quite touching me. The radiant light that has become so familiar to me permeates everything around us and I realize now that she *is* the light.

"Are you ready to come with me, Kitty Cat?"

I look past her and see myself lying in Jacob's arms as he sits next to the fireplace. My breaths are shallow and I can again feel a twinge of pain, the pain that has wracked my body for quite some time now. It is far away and dull. I shake my head. I cannot leave. Not without saying goodbye.

Struggling, I raise my head and meet Jacob's tear-filled eyes. His lips quiver as he fights to hold them in check and I place my paw on his cheek and tap him gently twice; something I have done to him since he was a baby. It never fails to make him laugh and it doesn't this time, although the laugh is a watery one. I nuzzle his chin with mine one final time, then allow myself to slip away. From a distance I see Jacob hugging my now lifeless body, his tears falling shamelessly upon it. Joe crosses the room to him and squeezes his shoulder gently, offering comfort. Their sorrow saddens me but I know it will pass. It is the cycle of life, as it should be.

Bekka is waiting.

I follow her and she returns me to the beautiful meadow. A sense of intense contentment and peace fill me. I know this is the house of the Creator and I will dwell here forever.

I am home.

About the Authors

Tom Gumbert lives near Cincinnati, OH with his wife Andrea (Andy) in a log home overlooking the Ohio River, in an area that was an active part of the Underground Railroad. Operations Manager by day, he has been writing for over a decade with an eclectic taste in what he reads and writes. www.tomgumbert.com

April Kautzman was born and raised in southwestern Ohio. She and her husband Phil reside with their cat and two crazy dogs near Cincinnati. In addition to writing, medieval history is one of her passions and it's on her bucket list to visit the Tower of London and as many castle ruins as she can find in the United Kingdom. She has known co-author Tom Gumbert for many years and was thrilled when he asked her to collaborate on *Nine Lives.* This is her first published work.

ALL THINGS THAT MATTER PRESS, INC.

FOR MORE INFORMATION ON TITLES AVAILABLE FROM
ALL THINGS THAT MATTER PRESS, GO TO
http://allthingsthatmatterpress.com
or contact us at
allthingsthatmatterpress@gmail.com

www.ingramcontent.com/pod-product-compliance
Lightning Source LLC
Chambersburg PA
CBHW060811250626
47162CB00005B/1738